WELCOME TO
WEIRDSVILLE

This

Dog Eat Dog

SAٰ
2.2

To re

WELCOME TO WEIRDSVILLE

Happyland

Ghostschool

Dog Eat Dog

WELCOME TO
WEIRDSVILLE

Dog Eat Dog

I. M. Strange

LITTLE, BROWN BOOKS FOR YOUNG READERS
lbkids.co.uk

LITTLE, BROWN BOOKS FOR YOUNG READERS

First published in Great Britain in 2013 by Little, Brown Books for Young Readers

Copyright © 2013 by Working Partners

The moral right of the author has been asserted.

A CIP catalogue record for this book
is available from the British Library.

ISBN 978-0-34900-127-2

Typeset in Minion by M Rules
Printed and bound in Great Britain by
Clays Ltd, St Ives plc

Papers used by LBYR are from well-managed forests
and other responsible sources.

MIX
Paper from
responsible sources
FSC® C104740

Little, Brown Books for Young Readers
An imprint of
Little, Brown Book Group
100 Victoria Embankment
London EC4Y 0DY

An Hachette UK Company
www.hachette.co.uk

www.lbkids.co.uk

With special thanks to Jan Gangsei

For my family, friends
and four-legged pals everywhere

CHAPTER 1

OK, I know everyone thinks their dog is the best. But with Scout, it's the truth. We picked him up a couple of years ago from an animal rescue centre. I don't know exactly what he is – some sort of mongrel. Fifty-five per cent Labrador. Forty-five per cent Boxer. One hundred per cent awesome.

I clicked my tongue and whistled. Scout came to a stop on the pavement, sat back on his heels and tipped his head at me.

"Good boy!" I handed him a treat from my pocket and scratched the soft spot behind his ears, just how he likes. He nuzzled his wet nose into my palm.

Not to be boastful, but I have a way with animals. I even taught my pet hamster Geronimo (may he rest in peace) how to do backward somersaults on command. I can train anything.

Well, *almost* anything.

My little brother, Freddy, strained against his reins and tried to pull me up the street. Yeah, I used to cringe whenever I saw some poor kid all tied up in a harness. Until Freddy came along. I'd much rather have left the little pest at home this morning, but Mum and Dad insisted I take him along to the pet shop.

"Hey, Leo!" someone yelled from behind.

I turned to see a girl from school, Evie, coming up

the pavement. Her fluffy little Bichon Frisé, Mandy, bounced ahead of her at the end of a hot-pink lead.

"Hey, Evie." I waited. Scout sat patiently at my feet. Freddy tried to sit on Scout.

Evie and Mandy were wearing matching pink sweaters and had their curly white-blonde hair done up in multi-coloured ribbons. Those two gave new meaning to the saying that people look like their dogs. Although, I suppose I have to admit that Scout and I aren't that different either. Same scruffy brown hair, skinny legs, and ears a little too big for our heads. Mum says I'll grow into mine. But I'm not so sure. I've seen Dad's.

Mandy twirled in circles around Scout, sniffing and tangling herself in his lead. Evie reached down and attempted to untwist the pink mess.

"You remember Mandy," she said.

"How could I forget?" I said, helping her untwist herself. "The first dog in dog show history to try to *eat* the obstacles instead of go over them."

"Humph," Evie said. "She'll do better this year. Won't you, wittle wovey-dovey?" She picked Mandy up, rubbed her face in the dog's fur and put her back down. Mandy immediately leapt after a bird.

At the end of the street, workers were busy stringing up a "42nd Annual Weirville Dog Show" banner across the front of the Weirville town hall. Evie nodded towards it.

"I take it you're competing tomorrow, Leo?" she said.

"I'm going to win," I said.

Freddy strained on his reins, lurching towards a piece of old chewing gum stuck on the pavement. I jolted forward, nearly losing my balance. Evie looked back and forth between Scout and my brother, and grinned.

"Oh yeah?" she said. "With which one?"

"Ha ha," I said. "You just wait. Scout and I have been getting ready for this *all year*. Haven't we, boy?" He woofed and wagged his tail. "We've got it in the bag."

"Is that so?" Evie said. "Care to make a little wager on that?"

"Sure," I said. "What?"

Evie shrugged. "How about fifteen pounds?"

I thought for a minute. Fifteen quid was nothing to Evie. But it was about two weeks' worth of chores for me. "Nah," I said. "Not high-enough stakes."

Evie twirled a blonde curl around her fingers and smirked. "OK, I know," she said. "If I win, I get to give your scruffball a makeover."

"A makeover?" I took a look at Mandy. Her head was sagging under a giant sparkling diamante collar. She wore a little skirt covered in five layers of ruffles. Fantastic. If Mandy won, Scout would end up looking like a celebrity Chihuahua.

But Mandy wasn't going to win.

"You're on." I held out my hand. "And if – I mean, *when* – I win, your little pink princess spends a week in Leo's Doggy Boot Camp, learning some manners."

"Deal." Evie shook my hand. "So where are you headed anyway?"

"Pet Village," I said. "To buy dog food."

"I'm going there too," Evie said. "Mandy needs some new accessories for the show."

We walked down the high street to the pet shop. An animatronic dog stood guard outside. I think the thing used to be white, but after years of kids stroking it with their grimy hands, it had turned a weird shade of grey. Dried-up chewing gum was stuck in the eye sockets. We walked inside. The place was small, but it had pretty much everything you could ever want. Dogs barked, birds chirped, cats miaowed, hamsters and guinea pigs ran in circles in little cages. It smelt like dog chews, bird seed, and wood chips.

I squeezed between tall shelves filled with pet gear and baskets of toys. Scout trotted obediently next to me, tail wagging. Freddy, disobediently, tried to climb a cat tree. I pulled him back and headed towards the dog food, passing a huge display of PetMunch. Rows of shiny silver cans were stacked on a table, with a life-size cardboard cut-out of Herman Munch's pet whippet, Diablo, perched in front. He was a scrawny thing, white from head to toe, with the exception of a small black patch on his skeletal chest. His long red tongue drooped from his mouth. Pretty much the last dog you'd want advertising dog food. Or anything, for that matter.

"Hey, Evie." I pointed at Diablo. "Think Mr Munch will enter him in the show again this year?"

"He'd be crazy to," Evie said, leaning over to adjust Mandy's hair ribbons. "Only thing *that* dog's ever going to win is an ugly contest."

"Ugly contest!" something squawked back.

"Who said that?" Evie said, frowning at the rudeness. She poked her head around the corner, smiled, then waved me over. "Check it out."

A red, green, and blue parrot stood on its perch in a hanging round cage.

"Cool," I said. Scout looked up and woofed.

"Tweet, tweet!" Freddy yelled and flapped his arms.

"Tweet, tweet," the bird mimicked.

Evie stepped closer to the cage, looked back and gave me a sly grin. "Dare you to stick your finger in there!"

"What?" I said. "Why would I want to stick my finger in there?"

"You're the one who's always saying you're so great with animals, Leo," she smirked. "Prove it."

I raised an eyebrow.

"Are you chicken?" she said.

"No." I put the leads in my left hand and poked my right index finger between the metal bars of the cage. "Here, little birdie!" I whistled and held my breath, hoping the thing wouldn't bite me. The parrot swung back and forth, back and forth, watching me with its beady eyes. I relaxed a little. "That's right," I grinned sideways at Evie. I'd show her who was great with animals. "Come here, little birdie." The little birdie leaned forwards . . .

And snapped its hooked beak at my finger.

"Whoa!" I yanked my hand away and tumbled backwards. The leads slipped from my grasp as I fell over and crashed into something. I heard an "Oof!" followed by the unmistakable sound of cans clattering to the floor. Mandy barked and Evie started giggling. Scout ran to my side.

I scrambled to my feet and turned around, straightening the toppled cut-out of Diablo. The shopkeeper lay next to the PetMunch display, blinking from behind a pair of crooked glasses. A large box sat upside-down on his lap and cans had spilled about his feet. "Sorry!" I reached out a hand and helped him up. "Didn't see you there."

The shopkeeper glared at me and stood, smoothing

his hair and adjusting his glasses and nametag. He surveyed the mess and sighed. "Now I've got to start all over again." He began picking up cans and stuffing them in the box, muttering to himself.

"Let me help," I said. I grabbed a can from the floor and read it. *New Improved PetMunch*. Diablo was on the front, but something looked different about him. It wasn't just the green and red superhero cape, or the stupid flying pose he'd been put in. It was his eyes. The way they seemed to be staring at the camera. They looked almost ... well, sinister. A little chill crept up my spine and I dropped the can in the box.

"What is this anyway?" I asked. I never bought PetMunch – it was full of disgusting fillers. Scout may be a mongrel, but he's still worth the good stuff.

"Something we just got yesterday from the PetMunch factory," he said. Then he sighed. "But now they want it back. Been recalled." I continued piling cans into the box. Scout sat quietly next to me. I could see Freddy out of the corner of my eye, jumping up and down, trying to grab a toy mouse off a high shelf.

"Freddy," I said. "Calm down."

He ignored me, of course. Evie sidled next to me.

"Nice move, Leo," she said.

"You could help," I said. "That whole finger in the cage thing was your idea."

"Nobody said you had to do it," Evie said while Mandy strained on her lead, trying to lick the bottom of the shopkeeper's upturned boot.

"Gross." Evie gave Mandy's lead a tug. "Stop it." Mandy just kept pulling until she was lifted upright, pawing the air directly in front of her face.

I swear I only looked away from Freddy for a split second, but when I turned around again, he was eating something off the floor. It took me another split second to notice the can of PetMunch, smashed open, and the globs of disgusting brown dog food smeared over the tiles. "Freddy, no!" I shouted.

I lurched towards him, a voice in the back of my mind saying, *Mum is going to kill me for this!* I grabbed Freddy by his small shoulders.

"Spit it out!" I gave him a little shake. "Come on, Freddy! Spit it out!"

He swallowed hard. Then grinned. Little dribbles of artificial gravy oozed from the corners of his mouth, down his chin and onto his favourite Power Trucks T-shirt. I tried not to gag.

"Ewwww!" Evie said. "Not only has your brother eaten dog food – he's eaten *recalled* dog food."

I picked up a can, wondering what was wrong with it. Maybe it was just a little past its expiry date or something. I couldn't find any sell-by information, though. Freddy waggled his head and licked his lips.

"Woof!" he said.

I groaned. Well, he looked all right. Hopefully he wasn't going to puke all over the sofa later. I'd never hear the end of it.

"You are so weird," I muttered and reached for his reins. But just then, a post van rumbled down the street outside. Freddy cocked his head up and sniffed the air. Before I could get hold of him he let out a mighty bark, way louder than the little woof he'd just produced. He slipped free of my hands and bounded out of the shop on all fours, reins skittering behind him.

I tried to yell for him to come back. But I was drowned out by the sound of horns honking, people screaming – and the unmistakable screech of tyres skidding out of control on the road outside.

In an instant, Freddy's life flashed before my eyes. I raced for the door, heart pounding, palms sweating, terrified of what awaited me on the other side.

CHAPTER 2

Evie, Scout and Mandy charged out of the shop behind me. My brother was running on all fours up the middle of the road, barking at the post van. Several cars had stopped at strange angles, drivers leaning from the windows and shouting. Others tried to weave through the chaos, honking wildly. My heart pounded. One wrong move and my brother would be flattened.

"Freddy!" I dodged into the road and grabbed his

reins, pulling him back to the safety of the pavement just as a car whooshed past. "What is wrong with you? You could have been hit!" I said, panting.

Freddy tilted his head to the side and looked at me.

"I've had it with you, Freddy," I said. "When Mum hears about this, you can kiss your toy cars goodbye for the week."

Freddy barked.

Ugh. What was with him? Yesterday he was a cowboy, before that a ballerina. Now a dog. Were all three-year-olds this weird?

I gave Freddy's reins an annoyed tug – admittedly a little harder than usual – and turned to head back into the shop. Scout trotted next to me. But instead of following, Freddy barked again and pulled against the reins. They snapped in half. I stared in shock at the remains dangling from my hand.

"Freddy!" I shouted.

"Woof!" he yelled and scampered off, veering into an alley and sniffing the ground. If he'd had a tail, I'm sure he'd have been wagging it.

I groaned and tapped Scout. "Come on, boy. Let's get Freddy."

Once again, Scout and I took off after him. Evie and Mandy followed. The alley was dark and narrow, with empty boxes stacked in haphazard piles on each side. It smelt like three-day-old fish. A rat scampered from a rubbish bin.

"Freddy!" I said. "Where are you?"

Freddy woofed again and disappeared around the corner. I caught up in time to see him barge through a pitch-black door covered in bars. It squeaked on its heavy iron hinges and slapped shut. I ran towards the door and stopped short. Cobwebs hung from the edges. There was a "No Trespassing!" sign stuck in the middle of it.

Scout stopped and looked up at me.

"He couldn't run into a sweet shop, could he?" I muttered as I reached for the handle.

"You sure you want to go in there?" Evie said. She fiddled with her hair ribbons and wrinkled her nose.

"Mum won't be too happy if I come home without Freddy."

"It looks a little … dirty," Evie said.

"Now who's chicken?" I asked, then added some clucking noises.

"Am not," she said. "I just don't want to mess up Mandy's sweater."

"Whatever." I pushed the door open and ducked inside. Evie stayed right behind me.

"Hello?" I said. "Anyone home? Freddy?"

No one answered. The room was dark and gloomy. A single light bulb hung from the ceiling, swaying back and forth. It cast dim light into the shadows, briefly illuminating what looked like . . . a set of eyes? I jumped back and nearly knocked Evie over.

Scout and Mandy both began to whimper. Evie stepped beside me. Her shoulder trembled next to mine.

"Leo, this place is creepy," Evie said. "And it smells horrible. Where are we?"

I squinted as my eyes adjusted to the darkness. Rows of shelves lined the walls, all crammed with weird, antique-looking things. There were dusty figurines with mottled paint, old timepieces, and a row of pointy rusted metal contraptions that looked like medieval medical instruments. I shuddered. But that wasn't even the worst part – mostly, there were animals. Dead, stuffed animals with glass eyes staring down at us silently from everywhere. I would've given anything for the miaows and barks of the pet shop to break the horrible silence.

"Freddy!" I said, in a loud whisper.

Nothing. What was he pretending to be now? Deaf?

I took a cautious step forward. The floorboards creaked beneath my feet. Scout hung back. "It's OK, boy," I said, and gave his lead a little tug. But he wasn't convinced. He just crouched low and watched me. Evie stroked Mandy's trembling head.

"I don't think he's here," she said. "Maybe we should go, too, before someone comes in."

Just then, I heard something that sounded like heavy footsteps clunking up a set of stairs. A tall, thin man rose inch by inch from some sort of trap door in the floor behind the counter. His hair was jet black, his

21

skin pale. Shadows clung to the gaunt hollows of his cheeks. A threadbare suit hung from his angular shoulders and a narrow tie was wrapped tight around his neck.

He tipped his black top hat and smiled, showing off a row of pointy yellow teeth. "Welcome to Fortescue's Curiosities. I am Mr Fortescue," he said in a high-pitched, sing-song voice. "May I help you find something today?"

"Actually, I'm just looking for my little brother," I said. "Have you seen him?"

"I have not." He smiled joylessly. "I've been down-stairs, working on my creations." A wild look flashed across his eyes. Goosebumps crept along my arms. The man walked around the counter, lanky legs whooshing.

There was something terribly familiar about him, I

just couldn't place what. He stopped in front of Evie and leaned over, rubbing his long, bony fingers through Mandy's fur. Evie's shoulders tensed, but she managed what passed as a polite smile.

"What a lovely little dog," the man said. He reeked of mothballs and formaldehyde. "Perhaps I can stuff you when you die?"

Evie twisted her body to the side, and pulled Mandy from his grasp. "I don't think so!" she said, grimacing.

"A shame," the man said. He reached out his hand again.

Mandy snarled and snapped at him.

"Tsk, tsk!" the man said, waving a bony finger in front of Mandy's nose. "No manners whatsoever! Mummy should teach you better!"

I pulled Scout's lead and started walking slowly

around the shop, between shelves of dead stuffed things and rusty gadgets covered in cobwebs. The sooner I found my brother and got out of this place, the better.

"Freddy," I said. "Where are you?"

I'd made it halfway across the room when an old, yellowed book sitting on the counter caught my eye. It was propped open to a page entitled "Animal Magick". I leaned in for a closer look. In a flash, the shopkeeper was there. He lifted his bony hand and slapped the book shut. Dust puffed from the edges.

"What was that?" I said.

The shopkeeper narrowed his eyes at me and raised his pencil-thin black eyebrows. "Nothing a boy like you needs to know anything about. Now, is there anything I can help you with?"

"Yeah, like I said before. My brother."

24

"I thought we had established that your brother is not here," the man said, that awful sneer creeping across his face. He had a strange formal way of talking, like he'd learned to speak English in the nineteenth century.

Scout sniffed the air and pulled at his lead.

"What is it, boy?" I said. "Can you smell Freddy?"

He tugged again and pointed his nose towards a display behind the counter. I followed his gaze. A hamster sat on a low shelf. A brown and white hamster, with circles of brown around his eyes. He looked just like . . .

"Geronimo," I said in a whisper.

A pang of sadness crept across my chest. I really missed my old hamster.

I stepped closer. The stuffed hamster had been glued in a running position to a piece of jagged wood, one paw poised unnaturally in the air. His mouth was propped open as if he was snarling at some unseen foe. His top front tooth was chipped.

Wait a minute.

That was the same tooth Geronimo broke trying to eat one of Grandma's "special" toffees last summer. I squinted for a better look. On his left side I could make out a faint mark – right where Freddy had decided to give Geronimo a purple leopard spot with permanent marker.

"Hey!" I spun around. "That's my hamster!"

"Pardon me?" the shopkeeper said. He was now standing by a stuffed bird, pretending to dust it while he watched us. "Your hamster?"

"Yeah!" I said, pointing at Geronimo and feeling myself turning red with anger. "That's him, right there. See? Same white stomach and chipped tooth.

Why do you have him? I only just buried him in the pet cemetery."

The shopkeeper stared at me as if I was mad.

"Then in the pet cemetery I'm sure he lies," the man said. The corners of his mouth twitched up briefly into a smirk. "Unless you think he unburied himself and walked here?"

OK, so maybe it wasn't Geronimo. Maybe it was a huge coincidence, and lots of hamsters chipped their teeth and had unfortunate run-ins with felt-tip pens. But I didn't think so. And if this guy would lie about a hamster, what was he hiding about Freddy?

"Tell me where my brother is!" I pointed a shaking finger at the trap door behind the counter, less angry and more scared now. "Is he down there? Are you planning to stuff him, too?"

The shopkeeper leaned across the counter and stared at me, a terrible glint in his black eyes and laughed. "Hmmm ... Stuffing humans. That had never occurred to me."

I shrank back. Scout snarled, teeth bared. "Freddy!" I yelled. "Are you here?"

A bark came from somewhere across the room.

"Leo!" Evie said. "This way! I've found him!"

I dashed around the counter, past the shopkeeper, towards Evie's voice. She was standing in front of a stuffed cat that was perched on a shelf in a dark corner of the shop. Its glass eyes glowed yellow. Freddy was down on all fours, growling at it.

"Freddy, there you are," I said. "Don't you run off again. Ever!" I reached for what was left of his reins. But before I could grab hold, Freddy launched himself at the cat. It crashed down to the floor.

The shopkeeper crossed the room in long strides. "What are you children doing to my precious displays?" Freddy leapt forward and tried to bite the cat.

I scooped my brother up under my arm. He licked my cheek as we ran towards the front door. "Freddy, that's enough," I said. "How about pretending to be a human for once?"

Scout scrambled alongside with Evie and Mandy. A bell jangled on our way out. I could hear the shop-keeper yelling behind us.

"Oh, my beautiful cat!" he wailed. "You horrible children are never welcome in Fortescue's Curiosities again!"

We raced down the alley and stopped at the corner, panting.

"As if I'd even want to go in that creepy place

again," Evie said. She swatted at her pink sweater as if it had been covered in cobwebs and stroked Mandy's head.

"Me neither." I looked back down the alley at the strange little shop. There was no sign outside – only a number etched onto the door. *Thirteen.* I gulped.

"Except," I said.

"Except what?" Evie said.

"I think I saw my hamster in there," I said with a shiver. "Stuffed. On a shelf."

"That doesn't make any sense," Evie said.

"No, it doesn't." I tried to tell myself I was being ridiculous. But I couldn't stop thinking about it.

"It was kind of dark in there," Evie said. "Could have been any hamster."

"Maybe." I reached down and rubbed Scout's head. I couldn't take it. My pets were more than just pets to me. They were like family. "I have to know if that was Geronimo," I said.

"And how do you plan to do that if you're never going back?" Evie said.

"Well," I said. "I can think of one other way to find out . . ."

CHAPTER 3

When the alarm clock buzzed, I bolted upright, heart thumping, and switched it off. Midnight. Maybe Evie was right. Maybe this was crazy. But no, I needed the truth. A tingle of anticipation crept over my body as I kicked off the covers.

I flicked on the light and lifted a newspaper cutting from my bedside table. Geronimo stared back at me in black and white, his chipped tooth clearly visible. I skimmed the article next to the photo:

Local boy teaches hamster to obey commands

Geronimo is not a dog. But don't tell him that. This two-year-old hamster has been trained by his owner, twelve-year-old Leo Martin, to roll over, beg, and even chase his own tail.

I didn't really care if Evie thought I was nuts. That dog of hers could learn a thing or two from Geronimo.

"OK, boy," I said, standing. Scout yawned, then uncurled himself from the end of my bed and hopped to the floor. "Let's go and find some answers."

I quietly pulled on some tracksuit trousers, slipped out of my room and tiptoed down the hall. Scout's collar jangled as we walked. I stopped and put my hand over it, casting a cautious glance back at Mum and Dad's room. I held my breath and waited, but no light came on. Phew.

"All clear," I whispered. Scout wagged his tail. I led him down the stairs, careful not to creak too loudly, and out of the front door. The cool air nipped at my cheeks. A light mist blanketed the ground, curling into ghost-like wisps and making the streetlights all weird and blurry. Fine time to head off on a cemetery expedition. Staying in my warm bed was starting to seem like a better plan. I hesitated a moment.

Scout barked and looked up at me expectantly.

"You're right, boy," I said. "We need to do this. We owe it to Geronimo."

I walked through the damp grass around the side of my house and pulled my bike from the shed. It was an old thing, with rusty spots and giant handlebars that were popular some time last century. But I didn't care. It suited me fine and got me where I needed to go.

I hopped on, undid Scout's lead and pedalled down

the pavement. With Scout running at my side, we raced down the empty streets, past rows of darkened houses, and up the steep hill that led to the graveyard. I was out of breath when I reached the top. Evie was already there, leaning on a shiny pink bike under the black-painted "Weirville Cemetery" sign. Mandy sat in a white wicker basket perched on the front. Glittery streamers hung from the sides.

"Nice bike," I called out. "Did it come with matching tiaras?"

"Ha ha," Evie said. "Got here faster than your hunk of tin, didn't it?"

"I live further away," I said, even though it wasn't true. Evie's house was nowhere near the cemetery. Or anything unpleasant. She lived on the opposite side of town, in one of those posh new houses in acres of garden with a big gate at the front.

I climbed off my bike, propped it against the cemetery's wrought iron fence, and peeked through the pointy black posts. Rows of white headstones lined the ground on the other side, glinting like jagged teeth in the moonlight. The pet cemetery was in the far left corner, tucked behind a row of yew trees.

I gripped Scout's lead and with a shaking hand pushed the front gates open. They creaked on their hinges. I tapped Scout's head. "Let's go, boy," I said. "Time to say hi to Geronimo."

We walked along the main path through the cemetery. Smaller paths led off it, snaking their way between the gravestones and disappearing into the darkness. Here and there I spotted wilted flowers and other makeshift memorials propped up against the headstones – framed photos, jewellery boxes, and faded drawings. I started walking faster. Scout scampered alongside, nose pointed straight ahead, ears pricked up on high alert.

Finally, we reached the sign that pointed up a small hill to the pet cemetery.

"This way," I told Evie and began climbing. She clambered after me.

"Ewwww, my shoes!"

I looked back to see her stumbling up, high-heeled boots sinking into the grass with every step. I shook my head. Only Evie would wear designer footwear to a cemetery. She pulled Mandy along, muttering, "Look out for the mud!" and "Gross, gross, gross!" every few seconds.

We reached the clearing at the top. Here, the graves were somehow more cheery, shaped like cats, dogs, and other pets. People had left chewy toys and children's sketches leaning against the headstones. I weaved through them towards Geronimo's grave at the back.

"Leo!" Evie hissed. "Hold on."

I stopped and tapped my foot. Scout came to my heel. "Look Evie, I didn't need you to come ..."

"No, look at this." Evie pointed to a large marble monument. I read the inscription. *Napoleon, beloved pet and fastest dog for miles around.* Napoleon was a retired racing dog who had taken top honours at the Weirville Dog Show for the last five years. Purebred greyhound. Perfect disposition. Obedient. And yes, fast – super fast. He was pretty much unbeatable.

"I didn't realise he'd died," I said.

"You know what that means, don't you?" Evie said.

"The world is missing an amazing dog?" I said.

Evie leaned over and adjusted Mandy's hair ribbons. "No, the field is wide open for the dog show this year."

"Did you just say that?" My jaw dropped. "Out loud?"

Evie shrugged. "It's true, isn't it?"

I supposed it was. I gave Scout another rub and nudged him forward. He shuffled along, nose pressed to the ground. We stopped at Geronimo's grave, a marble hamster wheel inscribed with his name. What I saw sent a chill straight down my spine.

The earth all around the headstone had been churned up into little clumps. Soil and grass lay every which way, like something had recently clawed its way in. Or out . . .

"Evie, look," I whispered. "This proves it! That creepy old guy must have dug him up." I felt furious.

Mr Fortescue was going to have some talking to do when I showed up at his shop tomorrow.

Evie's mouth twisted sideways. "Maybe it's like that because he's just been buried. You said it's only been a week, right?"

But I'd been extra careful to tidy the earth and grass when I'd covered his shoe-box coffin. I wanted his final resting place to be just right. This wasn't how I'd left him.

I sucked in a deep breath. "Well, I guess there's only one thing left to do," I said. I dropped to my knees and began shovelling away the loose soil with my hands. Evie just stood there. I looked up at her, perfect blonde curls silhouetted in the moonlight. "You going to help me, or are you just going to watch?"

"Well . . . " Evie held her hands out in front of her

face and inspected her long, pink fingernails. She looked back into the grave, grimacing. "I just got this manicure for the show tomorrow . . ."

"Oh, whatever." It was stupid to think someone like Evie would actually get dirty on purpose. I kept digging until I hit the little shoe box Geronimo was buried in. Hands trembling, I pulled it out. I could hear the chewy toy I'd put in there with him rattling around inside. Scout crouched next to me, sniffing the earth and snarling.

"Here goes nothing, boy." I counted to three and flipped the lid up.

The box was empty.

Only the toy remained.

"I don't believe it," I said. "That Fortescue really did . . ."

Evie grabbed me by the arm and yanked me to my

feet. She was a lot stronger than she looked. The box tumbled out of my hand.

"Hey! What are you doing?" I said. Geronimo's toy rolled across the grass. Scout chased after it and grabbed it in his teeth.

"Quick!" Evie said.

She dragged me around a huge gravestone in the shape of a horse. Her eyes darted left and right. "This will have to do," she said – and pushed me into the open pit behind it. Scout leapt in on top of me. Evie hesitated a moment, then pinched her nose and jumped in too, Mandy clutched in her arms. What was going on? One minute ago, Evie wouldn't even dig a tiny grave, and now she was throwing herself into one?

I stood and brushed earth from my trousers. I took the chewy toy from Scout's mouth, dropped it in my pocket and glared at Evie. "What did you do that for?"

Evie shook her head and mouthed, "Shhh!"

Click, clack, click.

"Get down, Leo!" Evie said, pulling my sweat-shirt.

Footsteps shuffled down the path, followed by a weird scraping sound.

Scratch, scrape, scratch.

"What is it?" I whispered.

Mandy bared her teeth and snarled.

"Quiet, girl!" Evie said, gripping the little dog tighter. I closed my eyes and focused on listening.

"It sounds like ... digging." Slowly, I stood and peeked around the horse's hind legs. The moon had slipped behind the clouds. All I could make out was the tall, shadowy shape of a man in a long coat and top hat standing over a grave – Napoleon's grave. My knees went weak. The man hoisted a shovel in the air and pressed it into the ground with his foot, tossing clumps of earth to the side.

Mandy began to growl again.

The man stopped, shovel poised mid-air.

"Who's there?" he said.

He turned just as the clouds shifted, casting a beam of moonlight across his gaunt face, hook nose, beady eyes, and black slash of a mouth. I tumbled back into the grave.

"It *is* Mr Fortescue!" I hissed. "This definitely proves it! He *did* dig up Geronimo. And now he's trying to dig up . . . "

Evie clamped her hand over my mouth.

Mr Fortescue jammed the shovel in the earth, tossing aside soil and singing to himself.

"Oh where, oh where has my little dog gone? Oh where, oh where can he be?"

He laughed as the metal end of his shovel clanked against something hard.

"Why, he's right here!" he said.

I struggled free from Evie's grasp. "We've got to stop him!"

A yapping interrupted me. Evie's eyes went wide. "Mandy?" she said.

"Well, well, well," said Mr Fortescue. "What have we here?"

Mandy was standing in the open, barking at Mr Fortescue.

Evie whistled. Mandy sat and wagged her tail. Mr Fortescue looked around the graveyard. "Now who would leave such a pretty little dog alone in an ugly place like this?" he said loudly.

"Mandy!" Evie choked out. "Run!"

"No matter!" Mr Fortescue said. "She'll do perfectly!" He reached down and scooped up the dog, tucking her beneath his overcoat, peering around the cemetery. Evie jumped up from behind the horse's tomb.

"Hey! That's my dog!" she yelled.

"I'm sorry, *your* dog?" The man's thin lips curled into a smirk. "What is it you children like to say? Finders keepers, losers weepers!"

"Give her back!" I yelled.

Mr Fortescue laughed and quickly strode away, dodging graves and headstones, overcoat billowing behind like a black cloud. Evie, Scout, and I chased after him. But Mr Fortescue was fast. Too fast. And he'd got too much of a head start. Before we could catch up, he was at the entrance to the cemetery, where a black van was parked at an angle in front of the gates. He opened the back door and tossed Mandy inside. She yelped as he slammed the door shut.

I sprinted through the cemetery gates just as he slipped into the driver's seat.

"Hey, stop!" I shouted.

The engine roared as he sped away. Taking Mandy with him.

CHAPTER 4

I ran after the speeding van until my chest heaved and I doubled over, panting. In the distance, Mr Fortescue screeched down the hill and turned right. I watched as the red rear lights receded and faded away. The night seemed darker now. And quieter. Evie jogged up alongside me.

"I can't believe this," Evie put her face in her hands. "Why did I have to come here? You and your stupid ideas!" Evie's eyes were welling with tears. "I'm never going to see Mandy again," she sniffed.

"Yes, you will," I said. Knowing I would feel exactly the same if it was Scout. "We'll catch him."

"How?" Evie said. "It'll be too late. Mandy will end up stuffed, sitting on his horrible shelf!" She wiped her hand across her nose and began snuffling again.

Scout barked and pawed the ground.

"What is it, boy?" I said.

He wagged his tail and put his nose to the road, where a fresh tyre mark was still smoking. I nudged Evie.

"Look, it's OK," I said. "Scout's picked up the scent. See?" I undid his lead and patted his head. "Go, boy. Find Mandy!"

Scout bolted forward. Evie and I climbed on our bikes and raced after him, down the hill and along the outskirts of town. Evie shifted gears effortlessly, going faster and faster. My bike's one gear was rusted in place, so I had to stand and pedal just to keep up. We continued on until Scout reached a junction. To the left, a paved road headed back towards the glimmering lights of the town. To the right, a gravel track barely wide enough for one car snaked deep into a wooded area I'd never seen before. Scout slowed, sniffed the ground, and turned right.

We pedalled cautiously down the narrow road, Scout still leading the way. Scraggly trees lined either side, bare branches twisting overhead and clawing the night sky. It was eerily quiet – not a sound except the stones crunching beneath the bicycle tyres, our laboured breathing, and Scout's panting. No birds chirped. No squirrels chattered. Nothing. It was like we were the only living creatures for miles.

The road came to a dead end in an empty car park. Evie skidded to a stop just outside the entrance.

"Whoa," she said.

"Whoa is right." I stopped next to her and got off my bike, leg muscles twitching.

Beyond the car park loomed the dark outline of some sort of huge factory. It looked like something straight out of an old horror film – faded brick, and rows and rows of small square windows covered in security grilles. Smoke puffed from tall black chimneys. A metal fence surrounded the whole thing, topped with twisted barbed wire.

"What is this place, Leo?" Evie said with a shiver.

I wasn't really sure I wanted to know the answer to that question. There were no signs anywhere. But whatever it was, it was important enough to need a security guard. He sat in a small cabin, just inside an open gate in the metal fence, reading a newspaper and sipping from a polystyrene cup.

And just beyond that, Mr Fortescue's van was parked. Lights began to flicker on inside the building.

"Mandy!" Evie said. "He's taken her in there!" She jumped off her bike and was about to run forward, but I grabbed her in time.

"Wait!" I hissed. "We need to work out how to get past that guy."

The guard stopped reading and peered over the top of the paper. Evie froze. Scout crouched down low. We waited. Holding my breath, I edged slowly forward. Evie had managed to dodge behind a bush. The guard was now leaning back, watching something on a small screen in front of him. Light flashed across his face and he laughed.

I checked the fence. No way to get over. Not without losing an eye at least. We had to distract the guard somehow. I knelt down next to Scout and pointed towards the cabin.

"What do you think, Scout?" I said.

Evie rolled her eyes. "Why are you asking him?" she said. "He's a *dog*."

"So," I said. "He's cleverer than most people I know."

I rubbed Scout's head and watched the guard open a lunch box and unwrap a sandwich. The guard took a bite, then rested his arm on the cabin's open window frame. The sandwich dangled loosely in his hand. Scout sniffed the air, tail wagging, and nudged my arm with his nose.

"Good idea, boy!" I said. I undid his lead and pointed. "Go get that sandwich!"

Scout charged forward. Before the guard could even realise what was happening, Scout had snatched the sandwich from his fingers.

"Hey! What?" The man jerked up, his blue hat toppling from his head. He looked around and caught sight of Scout, running back out of the gate, sandwich clutched between his teeth.

"Get back here, thief!" the guard yelled, chasing after him. As Scout led the man further away from the open gate, I motioned to Evie.

"Now's our chance!"

We left our bikes in the gravel road, ran across the car park, and through the gate. Scout was now over by the road. He dodged left and right. The guard lunged at him but missed completely and landed face first in the dirt. He jumped up, slapping debris from his trousers.

"Why, you little mongrel . . . " he said.

I slipped into the guard's cabin and searched the control panel. Lights, intercom . . . *gate!* I hit a red button. The front gate creaked on its hinges and began swinging shut. The guard spun around and looked at us, mouth open.

"What do you think you're doing?" he yelled.

I whistled to Scout. "Here, boy!"

Scout dropped the sandwich and raced towards the closing gate, the guard coming after him, arms outstretched. The gate was nearly closed.

"He's not going to make it!" said Evie.

"Hurry, boy," I yelled.

Scout scrambled as fast as he could, kicking up clouds of dust. He got through the gate just as it clicked shut. The guard slammed into it, eyes bulging, face red.

"Open this right now!" he said, panting. "Don't make me call for backup!" He patted his pockets. I glanced down. A walkie-talkie crackled on the desk in front of me. "What with?" I asked.

"Hey," the guard said. "Give me that!"

"I don't think so," said Evie.

The guard's face grew even redder. "You have no idea how much trouble you're in!"

The guard continued to yell and swear as Evie, Scout, and I ran up the brick steps to the factory's front doors. As we got closer, I could hear the low, grinding hum of machinery coming from inside. I hesitated for a moment at the double doors. They were the same pitch-black as Mr Fortescue's creepy little shop and covered in some sort of ornate iron-work, the letters "PM" inscribed in the centre.

"What do you think 'PM' stands for?" I said.

"I have no idea," Evie said.

Scout whimpered and pulled back.

I reached out a hand and grabbed the door handle. It vibrated softly beneath my fingers. What sort of factory was this? And why would someone want to bring an innocent dog here in the dead of night?

I wasn't looking forward to finding out.

CHAPTER 5

We stepped inside and found ourselves in a cavernous warehouse with endless rows of metal shelving, boxes stacked ten metres high on top. The air was cool and damp. Round fluorescent lights wrapped in wire glowed from the tall ceiling, casting strange shadows across the dusty concrete floor. The grinding noises were even louder in here – metal scraping on metal. Everything shook. There was no sign of Mandy – or anyone else, for that matter.

Evie chewed her thumbnail. "Who's running this place?" she said. "And what are they making at this hour?"

"Good question," I said. "Maybe we should have a look." I walked over to one of the boxes and lowered it to the floor. Scout's nose snuffled along the top as I ripped it open. Rows of some very familiar shiny silver cans were lined up inside. I turned one over and read.

New Improved PetMunch.

So *that's* what the "PM" on the gate stood for.

"PetMunch." I said to Evie. "That stuff the pet shop was sending back today. Why would Mr Fortescue be hanging out in a dog food factory? Weird, huh?"

Scout sniffed at the floor and began pulling against his lead.

"What is it, boy?" I said. "Can you smell something?"

Woof!

Scout pointed his nose forward. I gave him some slack on his lead and he started running. We hurried down the corridor after him, passing several empty offices, heading deeper into the building. The sound of churning machinery grew louder. The air was so cold I could see my breath. Scout scampered down a long corridor and came to a sudden stop just short of a heavy door.

"What is it?" I dragged Scout to the door and opened it. When I looked inside I had to hold back a retch. Scout tucked his head behind my knees.

The entire thing was some sort of walk-in refrigerator. But it was full – floor to ceiling – with animals. Dead ones. Lifeless tails, paws and snouts protruded from shelves, some still covered with clumps of dirt. I put my hand over my face and struggled to catch my breath.

"I bet these all came from the cemetery," I said, gagging. "You can tell by the soil."

"What sort of lunatic digs up dead animals and sticks them in a freezer?" Evie asked.

"Maybe he's going to stuff them."

"That's disgusting," Evie said. Scout whimpered.

"Or . . . " I had a sudden, horrible realisation. "What if he's putting them in the food?"

Evie turned a pea-like shade of green. "Why would he do that?"

"Who knows," I said. "Free meat?" I did always wonder what they meant by "fillers" and meat "by-products". Yuck.

Evie's eyes began to water. "Mandy!" she said,

poking her head inside the refrigerator. "Where are you? Come to Mummy."

We had to hope that Mandy hadn't been made into dog food. "Let's try this way." I turned and headed down another corridor, away from the grinding noises. Scout scampered next to me. Suddenly Evie sprinted past.

"Hey!" I called after her.

She stopped a few metres ahead, bent over and scooped something off the floor.

"Leo, look!" she said, holding the brightly-coloured thing up in the air. "It's Mandy's hair ribbon. She must be around here somewhere."

"Let me see that." I ran to her, grabbed the ribbon and held it under Scout's nose.

"Find her, boy!" With a wag of his tail, Scout barked and charged forward. We raced after him, barely keeping up as we skidded around corners and down more dim corridors that led deeper into the factory. Finally, we were getting somewhere!

Or not.

Just our luck, the corridor ended at a brick wall. On it hung an enormous framed portrait of Mr Fortescue sitting on a high-backed armchair.

"Look like anyone we know?" I said.

"Wow, totally." Mr Fortescue's hooked nose was tilted upward, black hair slicked back, top hat in hand. His other bony hand rested on a mangy-looking whippet of a dog with wiry white hair and a distinctive black patch on his chest. There was a can of PetMunch at his feet.

"But if he's actually Mr Munch, why does he go by Fortescue in town?" I said.

Evie scoffed. "Well, obviously he just uses the name

Munch to suit his career. I mean, who would want to eat 'Pet*Fortescue* dog food'?"

"Yeah, well PetMunch isn't that great, either," I said.

Beneath the portrait, a gold engraved plaque read: "Mr Munch, PetMunch CEO, and his prize-winning dog, Diablo."

Prize-winning? Now that was a stretch.

"Anyway, so much for your dog's amazing nose," said Evie. "He's led us down a dead end."

"I don't get it," I said. "He's never been wrong before."

I sighed and tugged on Scout's lead. But he didn't budge. He crouched on all fours and growled at the portrait. I knelt down next to him.

"What is it boy?" I asked, patting his head. As I did, I noticed a slight draught lifting the fur on his back. I ran my fingers through it. It was cold. And coming from behind the portrait. I jumped to my feet and began feeling around the edges.

"Have you lost your mind?" Evie said. "What are you doing?"

Scout sat up straight, tail wagging, and barked in approval.

"I think there's something behind here," I said. I felt around the side of the portrait and pulled. It wiggled, but wouldn't release. From this angle though, I could see the PetMunch can in the picture was ever so slightly higher than the surface of the painting.

It couldn't be, could it?

I ran my hand over the can and gave a push.

The can clicked into place. With a groan, the portrait rattled on its hinges and swung open. A blast of air rushed out, smelling just like the pet shop – all wood chips and bird seed. We were immediately greeted by a chorus of barks, miaows and tweets. Evie jumped back.

"What on earth?" she said.

Behind the painting was a dimly-lit room packed with animals in cages, stacked all the way to the ceiling. Dogs, cats, snakes, guinea pigs, birds. They slithered and squirmed and spun in their cages like mad. A large desk sat on the opposite side of the room with a nameplate reading "Herman Munch, CEO" perched on it. But the big chair behind the desk was empty.

"Looks like Mr Munch – I mean Mr Fortescue's office," I said. "Maybe we can find a clue to where he's taken Mandy."

CHAPTER 6

We stepped over a small ledge into the room. The picture swung shut and the room went dark. I ran my hand over the wall, found a light switch, and flicked it on. The animals went nuts again. There had to be a hundred of them, all crammed into cages barely big enough to stand in. It was horrible. Only a monster could do this to innocent creatures.

I walked over to a Jack Russell terrier cowering

behind a set of bars, big brown eyes looking at me pleadingly. I reached in and touched his head.

"It's OK, boy," I said. "We're going to get you out of here." I swallowed hard. "Somehow."

Evie sidled up next to me. "Hey," she said, peering into the cage. "Isn't that Watson? Won best of breed last year?"

I looked a little closer.

"Watson?" I said, and the dog jumped up and wagged his tail.

It *was* Watson. Weird. What was he doing here? There was a little placard taped to the front of his cage with the single word "Purity" written on it in black calligraphy. As I looked down the row of animals I saw they were all labelled with different qualities: "Strength" ... "Intelligence" ... "Speed" ...

Evie's hand flew over her mouth and she ran towards one at the end marked "Beauty".

"Mandy!" she said. "There you are! Don't worry, wittle baby, wuvvy dovey, Mummy's going to get you out of here. Yes, she is! Come here, my wittle sweetheart." Scout looked up at me, head cocked to the side. I shrugged back at him. I love him to bits, but you'd never catch me talking like that. Not in a million years.

Evie reached out to open the cage's latch, still babbling in a baby voice to Mandy. Behind me, I heard footsteps on the other side of the picture.

I leapt forward and grabbed Evie by the sleeve.

"Leo, what are you doing? You're going to rip my new jumper!" she said, trying to shake me loose.

"This is bigger than a jumper," I hissed. "Someone's coming!"

Evie blinked. "Mandy!" she said, still reaching her

hand towards Mandy's cage as the painting swung open. I yanked Scout and Evie behind the desk.

"Ah, it's time," said a man's voice. The animals went mad, barking, miaowing, and tweeting wildly. Scout lowered his head onto his paws.

Time for what?

Through the small crack beneath the desk, I could see a pair of black shoes caked with mud shuffling along the floor. They were connected to a set of long, skinny legs half-covered by a black overcoat. Evie's nails dug into my arms.

Mr Fortescue.

"Now, who's the special someone that's coming with me today?" Mr Fortescue said, rattling the cages. The barks and miaows turned to whimpers and screeches.

I heard a latch click and a door open. There was a

high-pitched yap and growl. Mr Fortescue cried out, "Ow!"

I peered out. Mr Fortescue stood there rubbing his hand. Mandy sat in the open cage in front of him, tiny teeth bared. Mr Fortescue reached out again and grabbed hold of her.

"Come on, you rotten little mongrel," he said. "We need a fresh batch for the competition. Time to go into the machine like a good girl." Mandy squirmed against him, but he just clapped a hand over her muzzle. "Don't make this any harder than it needs to be!" he said.

I stroked Scout's neck to keep him calm. There had to be a way to stop Mr Fortescue. As my fingers caught in Scout's collar, it gave me an idea . . .

I unfastened the lead from Scout's neck and held it up. "Evie, you distract him," I whispered.

Evie looked at me sceptically, biting her lip.

I shoved her forward. She stumbled to her feet, mouth open.

"Hey you!" she squeaked.

Mr Fortescue spun around, still clutching Mandy. "How did you . . . ?" he said, mouth dropping open.

I tapped Scout's nose. "Stay," I mouthed. I shimmied along the floor, lead looped like a lasso in front of me.

"I want my dog back!" said Evie, jutting her chin forward.

"This is getting tiresome," Mr Fortescue said. Mandy squirmed in his arms.

"Mandy, come to Mummy," Evie said and whistled. "I've got a biscuit for you!"

Mandy's ears perked straight up. She let out a yelp,

wriggled free from Mr Fortescue's grasp and leapt to the ground.

Mr Fortescue scrambled after her. He didn't even notice me running from the side of the desk. I threw the lead around his chest and yanked it tight.

"What the devil?" Mr Fortescue squirmed and tried to break free. "Get this thing off me!"

Evie shot forward and scooped Mandy off the floor. Then, she stomped her boot down hard on Mr Fortescue's foot. He cried out in pain.

"Maybe heels weren't such a bad idea, after all," Evie said with a grin.

I looped the lead around Mr Fortescue one more time and tied it firmly. He wriggled his arms to no avail. I began backing towards the door.

"You're coming with us," I said, tugging him to my side. "Straight to the police station!"

"Is that so?" Mr Fortescue said. He dug his feet into the ground, held firm, and stared over my head with his soulless black eyes. Then he smirked. "We'll just see about that."

I felt a draught of air behind me.

I turned slowly to see a tall, angular man dressed in black standing in the doorway, his hooked nose silhouetted against the corridor light. He leaned forward and swung the top hat from his head.

Evie screamed.

"Mr Fortescue?" I blinked, looking back and forth in disbelief between the two identical men. "Hold on, what?" I said. "There are two of you?"

The second Mr Fortescue laughed and pulled an antique-looking pistol from his overcoat. The shiny black barrel glinted.

"Twice the fun," he said.

74

"Greatness always comes in pairs," the man wrapped in the lead said.

"We're twins," they both said in unison.

"I'm Mr Munch," the man next to me said.

"And we have already met," the man in the door said haughtily. "*I'm* Fortescue. Now let my brother go!" He pointed the gun directly at me.

I dropped the lead. Mr Munch squirmed and shook his arms free. Scout sidled up next to me.

"Kids these days have no manners." Mr Munch smoothed out his black jacket. "Animals are so much better!"

"So true, brother. You should have seen what these horrible children did to my shop earlier today. Knocked my beautiful calico cat right from his shelf."

"Not the calico," Mr Munch said. "Mother's favourite!"

"Exactly. She did love cats so! Which reminds me," Mr Fortescue said. "What is it Mother always said? About the cat?"

"Yes! The cat!" Mr Munch said. "Curiosity . . . your speciality! What did curiosity do again . . . ?" He tapped the tips of his long fingers together.

Mr Fortescue grinned maniacally. "Why, killed it, of course!"

This was not looking good.

CHAPTER 7

Evie huddled beside me, clutching Mandy and burying her face in the dog's fluffy white fur. Scout stayed at attention, teeth bared at the twins.

Mr Munch crossed the room and stood next to his twin. Side by side, they were like mirror images. Actually, they were more like matching shadows. Dark and sinister. The only difference was the gun in Mr Fortescue's hand.

"Let us go," I told them.

"Oh, we'll let you go." Mr Fortescue looked sideways at his brother and smirked. "Won't we, brother?"

"Of course we will," Mr Munch said.

"You will?" I said, momentarily hopeful.

"We'll let you go ..." Mr Fortescue said.

" ... straight into the dog food!" Mr Munch added with a terrible laugh.

I stood up straight and tried to put on a brave face.

"You may want to think twice about that," I said. "Our parents and the police are probably headed straight here at this very moment."

"Oh, really?" Mr Fortescue said. "And how might they find you here, hmmm? Did you leave Mummy and Daddy a little note? Let them know you'd be roaming around a factory late at night?"

Evie squeaked.

"Didn't think so," Mr Fortescue grinned. "I admire

your cunning, though. Quite useful, actually. Pair it with that one's sense of smell . . . " He swung the pistol towards Scout, then raised it to Mandy. "And that one's prettiness . . . "

"Why, Diablo is sure to win the show!" Mr Munch clapped his hands together.

"What do you mean, Diablo will win the show?" I said. "What show?"

The twins snickered. "Let's just get on with it," Mr Munch said.

Mr Fortescue nodded and waved the gun. "This way," he said, motioning towards the door. I hesitated. Scout pawed the floor and growled.

"We're not going anywhere with you." I tilted my head towards the pistol. "That thing is probably some old relic from your weird shop. Probably rusted up a hundred years ago."

Mr Fortescue pointed the pistol at the door and pulled the trigger. There was an ear-splitting bang. Evie and I jolted back. The animals went berserk. Mr Munch looked aghast at the hole in the back of his portrait. Light streamed in.

"Now what did you go and do that for?" he said.

Mr Fortescue shrugged. "Simply proving a point," he said. "Besides, after Diablo wins, I think it's high time you commissioned a new portrait, don't you?"

"Ah, right you are," Mr Munch said. "That portrait doesn't do him justice, now does it?"

"Not at all." Mr Fortescue pushed a button next to the picture. The door swung open.

"Come along!" He held up the gun. "Don't make me use this again."

We walked back into the corridor. Mr Munch led

the way with Mr Fortescue – and his gun – following behind. Every step took us closer to the terrible grinding noises. Evie sniffled next to me. Scout stayed close to my legs, tail tucked under. Our death march continued until we reached a set of double doors and stopped. The noise here was deafening. Bangs and clangs and metal scraping on metal. Scout sank back on his heels.

"Oh, nothing to be frightened of, is there?" Mr Fortescue yelled over the clatter.

"No, nothing at all," Mr Munch laughed and kicked open the doors. Mud fell from his shoe.

The doors opened into a massive room. I could just make out the top of some sort of machinery, whirring and puffing. I searched desperately for a way out, but couldn't spot one.

"Enough dilly-dallying." Mr Fortescue shoved us

through onto a huge metal catwalk. We clanked across a series of walkways. Down below, a conveyor belt fed into a stainless steel contraption fitted with steaming pipes, and what looked like a large, open cauldron in the middle. At the far end, small silver cans toppled off the belt and into boxes.

"Leo, what is that thing?" Evie whispered.

"Must be where they make the food," I said. My legs wobbled and I nearly lost my footing.

"Now, now! Careful," Mr Fortescue said, prodding us forward. "Wouldn't want an accident!"

Mr Munch puffed up his thin chest. "That's right, brother!" he said. "Proud to say we've been 1,571 days accident-free here at the PetMunch factory. No diseases, deaths or dismemberments." He paused and snickered. "Unintentional ones, that is."

Scout howled. I reached down and touched his

head. Evie held Mandy's quivering little body to her cheek.

The Munch brothers forced us onto a balcony that looked directly over the machine. Mr Fortescue walked over to a control panel and began running his fingers over the knobs and dials, a weird smile on his face. I watched his grip on the gun relax ever so slightly. Maybe if I could distract him somehow, get him talking, I could knock it from his hands and we could make a run for it.

"Pretty impressive contraption down there," I said, trying to swallow my fear. "Did you invent it?"

"Why yes, I did," he said. "I like to think of myself as a man of innovation at heart, you see. My brother there is more of an entrepreneur—"

"Oh, you flatter me," Mr Munch cut him off. "But time is wasting."

"Yes, yes." Mr Fortescue turned to a book propped next to the control panel. "Now let's see here ... " He began flicking through the pages, stopping on one marked, "Animal Magick."

I couldn't believe it! The book from the shop. The one Mr Fortescue had been trying to hide. I sneaked a closer peek. It appeared to be some sort of formula illustrated with crude drawings of dogs, snakes, birds, and a series of strange swirls and markings. Mr Fortescue glanced up and caught me looking.

"What is that?" I said.

"You might call it a *recipe* book." He grinned. "And you're going to make the perfect addition ... "

I clenched my fists to keep from shaking. "What are you talking about?" I said.

"Haven't you worked it out yet?" Mr Munch said. "To make the perfect dog food takes all the right ingredients. A little protein, a little fat … plus a little … " He rubbed his hands together.

"Magic!" Mr Fortescue finished.

He ran his bony fingers lovingly across the book's pages. "I first learned of this particular formula on a journey to a remote rainforest. The local tribesmen would eat the meat of their prey to gain their skills and become better hunters, you see?"

It was too horrible! I watched the gun in his hand. I had to keep him talking. "Not really," I said. "Maybe you could explain it to me?"

"Why, it's simple," Mr Fortescue said. "We take animals with all the attributes we desire and put them in our food!"

"Of course, that's not quite enough," Mr Munch butted in.

"We also needed the spell," Mr Fortescue said.

"Took me years to track down. Finally found it in this book in a tiny shop in Vienna. Odd little man running the place ... looked curiously like a ferret ..."

"Is that why you wanted Geronimo?" I asked, eyes on the pistol. "His obedience?"

Mr Munch smirked.

"And that's why you were out at the cemetery trying to dig up Napoleon," Evie said. "He was fast. And my Mandy ..." She clutched her dog closer to her chest.

"Yes, pretty little thing," Mr Munch said, purring. "Now that's enough chit-chat. We need to feed Diablo this new batch before the big competition tomorrow."

Mr Fortescue slapped the book shut, pressed a couple of buttons on the control panel, and raised the gun.

We'd run out of time. I had to try something. I pulled a treat from my pocket and tossed it across the floor. Scout tilted his head at me quizzically. I mouthed, "Go!" and he shot off after it.

"What is going on now?" Mr Fortescue turned towards the commotion. In that moment, I made a lunge for the gun.

"Brother, look out!" Mr Munch yelled.

Mr Fortescue spun back around and jerked the gun above his head just before I could reach it. He grabbed me by the hair and tugged so I couldn't move. Evie cried out. Scout scampered back to my side. Mandy barked in the direction of the treat, still sitting on the floor untouched.

"Nice try," he sneered, then lowered the gun and pointed it at my chest. "Now down you go. And no more funny business!"

He led us down a set of metal stairs that led from the balcony to the factory floor. The huge machinery clanked, groaned, and puffed up ahead. I looked back over my shoulder. Mr Fortescue held up the gun and stared straight down the barrel at me.

"Look on the bright side," he said. "Circle of life and all that."

I shared a glance with Evie. I couldn't see a single way out.

We were about to become dog food.

CHAPTER 8

As we reached the conveyer belt, Mr Fortescue ordered us to stop. Keeping the gun trained on us, he reached down and grabbed a set of ropes from beneath the machine.

"Secure them," he said, tossing the ropes to Mr Munch.

"Gladly," Mr Munch said. "Time for a little pay-back!" He bound Evie's feet and went to work on her wrists, knotting the ropes tight.

"Ow!" she yelled.

"If you would cease squirming, it would be much simpler!" he said. And he shoved her sideways onto the conveyer belt. She landed hard on her back with a cry of pain, and the belt cranked her slowly towards the machine. Mandy sat on her chest, yapping.

"I don't want to die," Evie said.

"Oh, boo-hoo!" Mr Munch said as he grabbed another piece of rope and fastened it around my ankles. Scout growled and leaned back, ready to pounce. Mr Munch swung a black boot into his side. He yelped and skittered backwards.

"Don't you dare hurt him!" I shouted. My whole body shook with rage.

"Then tell the mangy mongrel to back off," Mr Munch said. "Or I'll break his scrawny neck."

"Scout, sit," I said, lip quivering. Scout obeyed,

looking confused and hurt. Mr Munch bound my hands while Mr Fortescue grinned, baring his pointy yellow teeth. He cocked the pistol and I swallowed hard. This was hopeless. As far as I could tell, our only chance for escape was to come out of the other end of this machine.

As dog food.

Mr Munch pushed me onto the moving belt. Scout hopped beside me and snarled at the Munch twins. The belt churned forward, heading towards a large, dark opening in the massive machine.

My heart was pounding so hard I could barely hear myself think. With a jolt, the belt lurched into a stainless steel tunnel, plunging us into darkness. I sat up and hit my head on the top. Something clanged and screeched up ahead, but I couldn't see a thing. I squeezed right behind Evie.

"Your phone," I said. "Where's your phone?"

"Back pocket," she said. "But I can't reach it with my hands like this."

"Maybe I can." I squirmed over until we were back to back, and stuck my hand in her pocket. The grinding of the machinery was deafening. I pulled the phone out, spun around and shone its light straight ahead. It reflected off something shiny and sharp.

Blades!

"Quick!" I yelled. "Duck!"

Evie and I pulled ourselves and the dogs down flat just as a pair of four-foot shears sliced through the air. They grazed the top of my head. A handful of hair fluttered across my shoulders.

"That was too close!" said Evie.

The belt turned a corner and the tunnel widened.

Hoses attached to the sides began puffing a fine dust all over us. It went up my nose and burned my eyes. Evie started to cough. I waved my hands in front of my face. There was something very familiar about the smell. Like Mum's shepherd's pie.

I stuck my tongue out and licked my cheek. Wait a minute. It wasn't dust. It was herb mix!

"They're seasoning us!" Evie said.

The belt jolted around another corner. Dead ahead, more blades whooshed back and forth across our path, a foot above the belt. I had to do something. Evie shuffled backwards.

I handed her the phone and shimmied forward.

"What are you doing?" Evie said. "Get away from it, you'll be killed!"

I kept my eyes fixed on the first swinging knife. Left, right, left, right.

"Not today!" I yelled. I lifted my bound hands.

In one swift motion, I felt the blade whoosh between my wrists, slicing the rope in half. The severed pieces fell to the conveyer belt. I bum-shuffled backwards and reached down to untie my legs. Scout licked my face happily.

"Leo, that was crazy," Evie said. "Seriously crazy!"

"But it worked, right?" I turned and unbound her hands and legs. Mandy yapped and nuzzled her head into Evie's lap. Behind me, the blades sliced and stabbed.

"Let's see if we can get back out the way we came," I said.

We quickly crawled against the forward motion of the conveyor belt. But it was useless. In an instant, the belt lurched and sped up, hurling us towards the slicing blades.

94

"Dodge left!" I said.

We grabbed the dogs and ducked to the left.

"Now right!" I yelled.

We dodged and weaved like a heavily choreographed dance troupe. I watched in horror as the sharp edges of the knives swung down and skimmed just past my shoulder. Once we were clear, the belt careened around a corner, plunging deeper into the hellish machine.

"Maybe we can just ride this thing out to the other side!" I yelled over the spinning gears and grinding metal.

"Or not!" Evie pointed. There was light up ahead as the conveyor belt sloped down towards a large cauldron, open at the top, making strange crushing sounds. A piece of rope tumbled in, sending tiny shards of twine back up in the air.

A meat grinder.

Evie and I looked at each other, eyes wide. Without a word, we turned around and scrambled with all our might in the other direction, back towards the blades, pulling our dogs along. But the belt was too fast. As hard as we tried, we just kept inching closer and closer to the churning machine.

"We're going to die," Evie wailed. "And I won't ever get those pearl earrings Mum promised me."

Pearl earrings? We were about to be ground into dog food and Evie was worried about jewellery? That's when it hit me.

I sat up and grabbed Mandy from Evie's arms. "I know what to do. We'll jam the thing."

"Not with my dog, you won't!" Evie said, trying to snatch Mandy back.

"I don't want your dog!" I said. "Just this!"

I yanked the sparkling diamante collar from her neck and chucked it into the grinder.

There was a loud sputtering noise and the grinder let out a strange groan. But the belt lurched forward. Scout's hind legs slipped off the edge, dangling over the razor-sharp blades. He howled as the grinder clicked and popped below him. I pulled him with all my might, managing to get him back up, just as the gears let out one final sputter.

And stopped.

The clattering ceased. I dropped my head, breathing heavily, arms still wrapped around Scout's neck.

"It's OK, boy," I said. "We made it." He licked my face.

"I can't believe you did that!" said Evie. She looked furious.

"What's the problem?" I said. "It was just some tacky diamante collar."

Evie blinked slowly and took a deep breath. Mandy was a vibrating ball of fur on her lap. "No it wasn't, Leo," she said. "Those were my grandmother's *vintage Cartier diamonds.* I had them specially mounted. They were worth thousands."

"Oh." I pulled away and peeked over the edge. The remains of Mandy's collar sparkled against the steel. "Well, surely it's better than being minced?"

I couldn't quite hear what she said then but it sounded like, "*Only just.*" She started crawling back the way we came.

"Hey," I said, going after her. "Don't I even get a 'thanks'?"

Evidently not. We dodged around bends, ducking beneath the now-motionless blades. When we reached the end, I stuck my head out a fraction and looked around. The twins were rushing about, pointing and yelling to each other. One stood on the balcony over-head, the other walked along the side of the machine.

"What is going on down there?" Mr Fortescue yelled from the balcony. "Can't you fix it?"

"You tell me," Mr Munch said as he scurried along the machine. "It's your invention."

"Never had a problem before," Mr Fortescue said. "Maybe those children were too big!"

"Nonsense," said Mr Munch. "We did that St Bernard last week."

I glanced back at Evie. "Get ready," I whispered. "When they're not looking, we'll slip out of here, OK?" She nodded.

I watched Mr Fortescue run along the gantry and peek into the machine. "Hold on! I see the problem," he said. "Down there ... the grinder, it's stuck." He tapped his foot. "Do something!"

Mr Munch ran to the other side, wielding a wrench. "Born first, doesn't make you the boss," he hissed.

"What was that?" Mr Fortescue yelled.

"Nothing, dear brother!" Munch said as he disappeared behind the massive grinder. I nodded to Evie.

"Now!" I whispered.

We slipped out of the machine and crouched on the floor behind the conveyer belt. It was covered in dust and flecks of fur. I shuddered to think what had passed through here before us. The twins were still bickering. I pointed towards a door on the opposite side of the room. "Over there," I whispered.

We shuffled slowly across the cement floor on our hands and knees. But we hadn't made it two metres before Mandy stopped and began to growl. The noise echoed through the cavernous room. I froze. Mandy snarled, eyes fixed on Mr Fortescue, and inched away from us.

"Seriously?" I said. "Can't you control that dog?"

Evie heaved a sigh. "Shhh, girl!" Mandy crouched low, ready to spring. Evie made a quick grab for her collar – but it wasn't there. All she got was a handful of empty air as Mandy leapt over the conveyer belt and bounded up the stairs to the balcony, straight at Mr Fortescue. He looked up in shock as Mandy, a flying cotton ball with teeth, came straight at him.

"Hey!" he said.

Mandy landed on the tall man and attached herself with a growl to his black collar. He shook left and right. Mandy just bounced around, refusing to let go. Mr Fortescue wobbled forward, steadying himself on the rail with one hand and raising the other to strike her. But Mandy was so small and squirmy, he kept missing.

101

"Get off me!" he yelled, finally getting hold of Mandy's fur. She tumbled down the front of his black overcoat, hanging by her claws, and dangled over the edge of the railing.

One wrong move and they'd both go head first – straight into the open grinder below.

CHAPTER 9

I clambered up the metal stairs while Mr Fortescue tried to shake Mandy loose.

"Get off me, you little mongrel," he yelled.

"Hey!" Evie said. "She's purebred Bichon!"

Scout bounded ahead, taking the steps two at a time.

"Scout," I said. "Get back here!"

He only ran faster.

"Scout! Stop!"

He completely disregarded me and charged along the balcony.

"Now whose dog won't listen, huh?" Evie said.

Scout let out a growl, jumped into the air, and knocked Mr Fortescue full-force on the backside. The tall man swayed back and forth on his long legs.

"Whoa!" he shouted, arms waving. Mandy clawed her way up the front of his jacket and fell to the floor – just as Mr Fortescue toppled head-first over the edge of the balcony.

At the same time down below, there was a sudden crunching whir. Mr Munch ran around the machine, the mangled remnants of the diamante collar waving above his head. "Look! I did it, broth—" He stopped mid-sentence, eyes wide in terror, as he watched his twin tumble into the open top of the churning grinder.

I screwed my eyes shut and turned away. But nothing could drown out the sound of bones crushing against metal and Mr Fortescue's final high-pitched shriek as he fell into the mincer.

I shuddered from head to toe.

"Noooooo!" Mr Munch wailed.

I opened my eyes. A torn piece of bloodied black fabric flew from the top of the grinder. I grabbed Evie by the hand. She still had her eyes pinched shut and was clutching Mandy to her chest, trembling.

"Come on!" I said. We raced along the metal walkways, Mr Munch's screams chasing us the entire way.

"Don't think this is over, you terrible children!" he yelled. "You will pay for this!"

We burst through the double doors back into the corridor. They banged shut, muffling the sound of the clanking machinery and Mr Munch's shouting. I stopped for a moment to catch my breath.

Evie was white as a sheet. "I think I'm going to be sick." She put her hand over her mouth.

"No time!" I said. Mr Munch's angry yells were closing in. We turned and hurried down the corridor, looking for the nearest way out, or at least somewhere to hide.

Somehow we found ourselves back in front of the bullet-holed portrait of Mr Munch. Mr Fortescue's wayward shot had caught his brother right between the eyes. I couldn't help but smile as I reached out and pushed the PetMunch can. The door swung open and the animals on the other side went mad.

"Quick," I said. "Unlatch them!"

Evie raced along one side of the room, flipping cages open, while I released the animals on the other side. In a mad flurry of fur and yaps, the kidnapped creatures ran, hopped, slithered and flew from the room. They scampered into the corridor and disappeared from sight.

"We did it!" Evie said.

"Yes!" I raised my hand for a high five.

Just then, an alarm blared. Red lights flashed in the corridor outside, bathing the cold grey walls in a crimson glow as if they were being drenched in blood.

"Security! Security!" Mr Munch's voice crackled over the speakers. "Intruder alert! Intruder alert! Release the hound!"

"'Release the hound'?" Evie said, her voice rising a notch. "What hound?"

"I don't want to find out," I said.

I leaned over and scratched under Scout's chin. "Outside, boy!" I said. Scout dropped his nose to the floor. We ran behind him and out of the room. Scout skidded around the corner into an unlit corridor. He turned again and we squeezed single-file through a narrow passage. With a bark and a tail wag, Scout led us to a large room on the other side – the warehouse!

"Well done, boy." I rubbed his head. We wasted no time running through the stacks of boxes towards the main entrance.

Woof!

I froze. Whoever that was, it wasn't Scout or Mandy. They had both come to a dead stop, teeth bared.

Woof! Woof!

I turned towards the low bark. A pair of red eyes stared back at me.

No, it couldn't be . . .

I recoiled as a huge white dog with a distinctive

black patch emerged from the shadows, growling. It paused twenty feet away.

"Diablo!" Evie gasped.

But he wasn't the scrawny whippet from the portrait any more. Whatever those Munch twins were feeding him *had* turned him into some kind of super beast. Muscles rippled beneath his fur. His legs were meaty and strong.

He dropped his head low and bared his teeth. A strand of slobber slipped from the edge of his mouth. He crouched down and pawed the ground.

Ready to pounce.

CHAPTER 10

"Let's just back away really slowly," I whispered. Evie nodded. But we hadn't gone two steps before Diablo sprang forward, jaws wide open.

"Run!" I said.

We turned and fled with the monster right on our heels, dodging back through the warehouse. I yanked down boxes to block Diablo's path. But he just leapt over them like he was running an obstacle course. I couldn't believe this was the same dog that couldn't even finish the race competition at last year's show.

Evie ran ahead, heels clicking on the cement, and yelled over her shoulder.

"Leo! I think there's a way out over there." She pointed towards a dimly lit "Emergency Exit" sign on the far wall.

"Yes!" I said. If anything qualified as an emergency, I was pretty sure this was it.

As we raced towards the sign, I yanked another stack of cans down. Diablo paused and sniffed, but then ran after us again. I could see the door, a narrow window at the top revealing the glow of the security lights outside. Al . . . most . . . there . . .

But as we got closer I saw something else – a heavy chain wrapped around the door handles.

"You've got to be kidding me," Evie said.

We spun around, backs pressed to the door, facing Diablo. We were trapped. The creature's red eyes glinted and he licked his snout.

"Stop looking at me like that," I said. "I am not a filet mignon!"

"No," Evie said. "More of a spam sandwich, I'd say."

"Seriously?" I said. "Is now the time?"

Evie chewed her lip. "I'm sorry," she said. "I have no idea how to act when I'm about to die."

"You're not going to die," I said. I looked around for something – anything – to stop Diablo. A stick. A net would do quite nicely. But, nope. All I could see were hundreds of boxes of stinky PetMunch. Hey, maybe that wasn't such a bad idea . . .

I grabbed a can and hurled it at the hard floor. It dented, but didn't open. I flung another, with the same dismal results. Diablo growled. Scout growled back – from behind my legs. Evie began rooting around in her pocket.

"Try this!" she said, handing me a pink, jewel-encrusted penknife with a funny little metal attachment poking from the top.

"What's this thing?"

"It's for clipping Mandy's nails, of course," she sniffed.

"Of course." I rolled my eyes. I jabbed the PetMunch can open and chucked it as far away as possible from where we stood. Grey chunks of food spilled down a wall. I grimaced. That stuff looked like three-day-old vomit. Smelt like it, too. But Diablo didn't mind. He turned away from us, bounded towards the glop, and lapped it up eagerly. We took our chance and hurried past him.

But as soon as Diablo had licked the last bit, he was

right on our tails again. I popped open another can and tossed it in his path, looking around the warehouse for somewhere to go. I couldn't keep throwing him dog food forever. Eventually I'd run out. Or he'd get full.

We had to trap him.

I turned away from the exit and bolted down the corridor that led deeper into the factory.

"Where are you going?" Evie said. "The way out is back there."

"You'll see," I said.

We ran on until we reached the door to the giant refrigerator full of dead animals. I hesitated a moment. Diablo was evil, but it wasn't his fault he'd been trained that way. Still, I didn't see what choice I had. I started to crack open a can of PetMunch and whistled.

"Here, boy!" I said.

Diablo streaked in my direction, teeth glinting.

I dropped the penknife. Oh no . . .

Diablo headed straight for me as I scrabbled on the floor. Bloodlust lit up his eyes.

I jammed the knife into the can again, prising up the lid with shaking hands. When he was ten feet away I opened the door and hurled the can into the freezer. Diablo gave a ferocious bark, opened his jaws wide, and leapt after the food. I quickly slammed the door shut, clicked the latch into place, and leant on the door, breathing heavily.

Scout woofed. There was a thud above my head. I jumped and spun around to see Diablo's glowing eyes framed by the small window at the top of the door. His paws scratched at the glass. He bared his teeth, revealing a chip in his front tooth. In a *very* familiar spot. My hand flew to my mouth.

"Geronimo?" I said with a shudder. I pictured my poor hamster and my eyes began to burn. "Mr Munch is so going to pay for this . . . "

"Yeah, yeah." Evie yanked my arm. "Right now we've got a bigger problem."

I turned to see the security guard from the cabin lumbering up the corridor. His trousers were still caked with mud and his shirt was half-untucked. He pulled a baton from his belt and swung it in the air.

"Think you can just take my dinner and lock me out, do you?" he said. He banged the baton against his hand. "You little menaces better think again."

"Uh-oh," I said. I fidgeted with the last can of PetMunch in my hand. "You don't suppose he'll eat this, do you?"

"No," Evie said. "But I have a better idea."

She grabbed the can, swung her arm behind her

back, and lobbed it straight at the guard. It sailed through the air, smacking him in the gut. The guard dropped the baton and doubled over.

"Ow!" he yelled.

We dodged past him, down the corridor, out of the open warehouse door, and straight to our bikes.

"Where did you learn to throw like that?" I said as we jumped on.

"What?" Evie grinned. "You think I'm all manicures and pink ribbons? I do have three older brothers, you know."

She plopped Mandy in the basket and we pedalled down the road at top speed. Scout ran alongside, tail wagging the whole time. Man, I love that dog. Nothing gets him down.

The sun was just beginning to creep over the horizon, sending rays of light between the branches of the skeletal trees. I checked my watch – nearly seven a.m. I couldn't believe it. We'd survived a night with two psychos in a freaky factory, avoided being turned into dog food, and rescued Mandy and a load of other innocent animals.

We were winners. Nothing could go wrong now.

CHAPTER 11

My house was closer than Evie's, so we decided to head straight there. We skidded to a stop in my driveway and Scout rolled with pure joy on the front lawn, biting at his feet. Evie stroked Mandy's head and pulled out her mobile.

I hoped she wasn't calling the police. Not yet, at least. I still hadn't worked out how we were going to explain everything. Or how we'd ever prove what the Munch twins were up to.

Evie tapped at the keypad with her fingers and shoved the phone back in her pocket.

"OK, I'm cool," she said. "Just texted Mum to say I got up early and came here to get ready for the dog show."

"The show!" I said. "That's it!"

"What's it?" Evie said, frowning at me.

"Our chance to put a stop to Mr Munch," I said. Evie still looked confused. "Remember what Mr Munch said? Something about feeding Diablo the special food before 'the competition'. He must have something planned for the show today. If we go, we can work out what it is – and catch him in the act."

"Good thinking, Leo!" Evie said with a nod.

We parked our bikes at the side of the house and crept silently through the back door into the kitchen, where we were greeted by fantastic barking. I stopped. Evie raised an eyebrow.

"When did you get another dog?" she said.

"Um, I didn't."

The barking continued. A voice came from upstairs. Mum. "Leo!" she shouted. "What scared Scout? Can't you settle him down?"

I shrugged. "Yeah, OK Mum," I called back.

The noise was coming from the dining room, so I headed in that direction. But instead of a dog, I found Freddy sitting at the table eating his cereal. He wasn't using a spoon. Instead, he had his entire face buried in the bowl. He looked up, milk dribbling from his chin, and panted.

My jaw dropped.

Freddy's entire face was covered in clumps of hair, his tongue had grown at least two inches, and his fingernails looked like claws. Long ones. A piece of oat bran fell from his fuzzy cheek.

Evie's mouth opened wide. "The magic dog food," she said. "He ate it yesterday!"

"No wonder Mr Munch had the stuff recalled," I said.

Freddy plopped his face in the bowl again. Mum ran into the room, clutching a thermometer.

"Oh, kids," she said. "You may want to stay clear of Freddy. He's got some awful virus or something. I've never seen anything like it! Hope it's not contagious."

I looked at Evie. "Um, yeah Mum, about that," I said. "It's not what you think . . ."

But Mum was too busy trying to stick the thermometer into Freddy's uncooperative mouth to listen.

"C'mon, Freddy," she pleaded. "Just let Mummy take your temperature. I'll give you a sweet after. I'll take you to the zoo!"

Freddy swung his head from side to side, snarling.

"What is the matter with him?" Mum said in an

exasperated voice. "He never turns down a trip to the zoo. He must be really ill!"

"Mum!" I said. "That's what I'm trying to tell you. He's not ill. Well, not exactly. He ate some bad dog food yesterday. This stuff Mr Munch has been making to turn his dog into a super dog."

"What?" Mum stopped momentarily, holding the thermometer in the air like a question mark. "What are you talking about? And who's your friend?" She blinked and tilted her head towards Evie, only just spotting her there.

"This is Evie," I said. "And she saw it, too – Mr Munch is making this awful food and—"

Mum cut me off. "Hang on, Leo, go back a minute. What did you say before? You let Freddy eat dog food? How could you?!" Mum grabbed my brother and wiped his milk-splattered face with her sleeve. "That does it. Freddy, we're going to see Doctor Franklin. Now!"

Freddy slipped from her arms and dropped on all fours, sniffing the edges of the carpet. He licked up a crumb. Mum struggled to grab him again.

"You might want to try the lead," I muttered under my breath as they hurried out of the house. "A really strong one."

Once they were gone, Evie and I collapsed into two empty chairs. Mandy curled herself up on Evie's lap. Scout flopped sideways at my feet. All I wanted to do was crawl into bed. But there was no time.

We had a madman to stop.

Evie and I parked our bikes in front of the town hall and led Scout and Mandy up the stairs. I paused at the top step, knelt down and rubbed Scout's head.

"We're going to do it, boy," I said. "We'll catch that bad man."

Scout woofed and licked my cheek. Did I mention that Scout's the best dog ever?

I stood to see Evie clamping a shiny new collar around Mandy's neck and adjusting the ribbons in her fluffy hair.

"What are you doing?" I said.

Evie shrugged and twisted her mouth to the side. "Well, if we're here, Mandy might as well have a chance to compete. We have been getting ready all year for this, right?" She cast a sideways glance at Scout – fur matted, clumps of dirt still stuck to his legs – and wrinkled her nose.

"Right," I said, looking my dog up and down. "Been getting ready all year ... "

I did my best to brush off the dirt caked on his legs

and smooth his fur with my hand. But he still looked pretty mangy. Oh well, there wasn't much I could do at this point.

"Ready?" I said.

Evie nodded. We walked together into the town hall. Dogs milled about everywhere, barking and sniffing at each other, while their owners combed fur, adjusted jackets, and practised commands. The entire place was buzzing, noise echoing through the main chamber. I could almost taste the excitement. In the centre of the room, show organisers were putting the finishing touches to the obstacle course and roping off separate judging areas. Spectators filed into seats along the walls. A judge's table sat on the stage up front, next to three elevated platforms for the show's top winners.

"Can you see Mr Munch anywhere?" Evie said.

I shook my head. We pushed our way deeper into

the crowd. I kept my eyes peeled for a flash of black top hat. But it was something else that caught my eye.

A bookie's table.

A bespectacled man sat behind it beneath a huge sign, shuffling money and betting cards. I read the odds listed above his head. Scout was there – 10 to 1. I smiled. Not bad for a mongrel. Mandy was 2 to 1. I kept going down the list until I reached Diablo. Dead last. Odds 300 to 1.

That's when it hit me.

"Evie," I said. "Mr Munch must be planning to bet on Diablo. With odds like that, he'll make a fortune if Diablo wins."

"We've got to warn the judges," Evie said.

We ran to the official's table, where Mayor Feversham sat, a pair of town dignitaries perched on either side. The mayor wore a dinner jacket, a bow tie, and a large red ribbon marked "Head Judge".

"Excuse me, sir," I said.

Mayor Feversham leaned over the table and cleared his throat.

"What can I help you with, young man?"

"We have something very important to tell you," I said. "About Mr Munch."

"Mr Munch?" he said.

"Yes," Evie jumped in. "He's been cheating! Feeding his dog Diablo special food to make him win."

"Special food?" the mayor said.

"Right," I said. "It's made from other animals and when Diablo eats it he gets all the attributes of the other dogs. You know, like super strength, speed, looks. Then he's unbeatable. Mr Munch needs to be arrested."

"And disqualified!" Evie added.

The mayor looked back and forth between Evie and me, face serious. Then he burst out laughing.

"Oh, that's a good one," he said, elbowing the judge next to him. "A special dog food that makes you invincible. I could do with some of that! What did you say it was? PetMunch?"

The other two judges joined in the laughter.

"But," I said, my face getting hot. "It's true! He's going to fix the competition and make a fortune betting on it."

The mayor caught his breath. "Of course he is," he said. "We'll be on the lookout for super dogs, OK? Won't we, Clive?" He poked the man on his other side and they all started laughing again. "Capes, X-ray vision, the lot!"

My shoulders dropped. How was anyone ever going

to believe us? Even I wouldn't believe us if I hadn't seen the whole crazy mess myself.

"Now you kids better get to your spots if you expect to compete," the mayor said.

Evie and I turned around and led the dogs back towards the staging area.

"This is crazy," Evie said.

"I know," I said. "But I can't see Mr Munch anywhere. Maybe he won't have the guts to show up."

"Maybe," Evie said. But then her eyes widened and she pointed to the entrance. "Or maybe he will."

The town hall doors swung open and banged against the wall. It felt like all the air had been sucked out of the room, like the calm before a storm. Mr Munch strode in. He had replaced his black overcoat with a blood red one. His black top hat sported a matching red ribbon. His eyes were two dark slits. The heels of his boots clicked on the marble floor and echoed through the cavernous hall. Diablo sauntered alongside, head held high. Mr Munch must have let him out of the giant fridge.

But now he looked even more fearsome than last night – ears pricked back, intelligent eyes surveying the room, muscles bulging. And if a dog could grin, he was grinning.

Wickedly.

CHAPTER 12

The other dogs in the room cleared a wide path for Diablo. Scout pulled back and whimpered.

"Don't worry, boy," I said, rubbing his head. Evie leaned over and whispered in my ear.

"Maybe we should call the police," she said.

"I don't know," I said. "What will we tell them? Look at the judges. They thought we were mad."

"We can't let him get away with it!" Evie said.

"No, we can't," I said. "We'll just have to get proof. Come on – let's follow him."

We walked along the edge of the room, past the other dogs and their owners, keeping an eye on Mr Munch and Diablo. Luckily they hadn't seen us. They headed right past the entrants' table to the bookie's stand. Mr Munch whipped a thick wad of cash from his overcoat and plopped it on the table, grinning. The bookie's eyes grew wide and he raised an eyebrow. His mouth moved and he licked his lips, counting the money. I could tell he thought Mr Munch was a complete sucker. If only he knew how wrong he was.

Evie pulled out her phone. "Maybe I can get a picture. Catch him in the act."

"Good idea," I said.

Just then, Mr Munch spun around. As his cold glare

133

found us, his face turned bright red and twisted into a scowl. My legs began to wobble as Mr Munch reached for something in his pocket. I could've sworn he mouthed, "You're dead!"

"Ladies and gentlemen!" a voice crackled over the loudspeaker. "Welcome to the forty-second annual Weirville Dog Show!"

A round of applause came up from the spectators, echoing through the room. Mr Munch dropped his hand back to his side and snarled in our direction, then disappeared into the crowd.

"If all entrants would please line up at the front, we'll begin the competition shortly!"

Evie, Scout, Mandy, and I were shoved along with a crowd of people and dogs.

"What are we going to do now, Leo?" Evie said.

I stood on my tiptoes, searching for Mr Munch's

tell-tale top hat. I finally spotted it at the starting area for the competition.

"We're just going to have to make sure Diablo doesn't win," I said.

"So that Mr Munch loses all his money," Evie finished.

We worked our way to the starting area while the mayor continued his introduction from the head table.

"The top three winners of each heat will go on to the final – our obstacle course!" He pointed to the centre of the hall where a series of tunnels, jumps, and bars were laid out. I felt the anticipation rise in my stomach. I knew Scout could get through that course in a flash. But was he fast enough to beat Diablo?

"Behind me," the mayor continued, "are the groups for each heat." Above his head, an electronic screen flashed dozens of names. I quickly scanned them. Scout, Mandy and Diablo were all in different groups. We had two chances to get a dog into the finals. This was it. The day I'd been waiting for was finally here. I reached over and tapped Evie on the shoulder.

"Good luck," I said. "May the best dog win."

Evie hesitated.

"What?" I said.

"About that," she said, twirling her hair. "I've been thinking."

"OK," I said, tapping my foot. The competition was about to begin. We didn't need a five-point penalty for lateness.

"It's just that Mandy isn't the best-behaved dog ... " Evie said. Mandy, as if on cue, began bouncing up and down and yapping at nothing.

"You could say that," I responded.

136

Evie took a deep breath, biting her lip. "And well, Scout is a bit of a scruffball ..."

"Hey," I said. "Is now really the time to start lobbing insults?"

"It's not that," she said. "It's just that we need to make our best effort if we're going to actually beat Diablo."

"What are you saying?"

"I'm saying, we should switch dogs."

"What?"

"Think about it," Evie said. "You're great at training animals – even hamsters."

"Yeah," I said.

"And I'm good at making them beautiful," she said. "I could do wonders with Scout. If you'd let me."

I took a long, hard look at my dog. With his prominent ears and fur still mottled with dirt from last night's adventures, even I had to confess he wasn't exactly show-dog material. Mandy, on the other hand, looked like she'd spent the entire morning lounging at a spa.

"You do have a way with grooming," I admitted.

"So we switch," Evie said. "Problem solved!"

My heart sank a little. "I don't know," I said. Scout looked up at me with his big eager eyes. His tail flicked back and forth on the floor. The fact was, we'd been working so long and hard together, it was pretty rough to consider letting him go. Mandy leapt up and tried to snatch a biscuit from the hand of a guy walking past. I shook my head. Hopeless. I wasn't sure even I could do anything with her. Not in five minutes.

Evie sighed. "Have you got a better idea then?"

Across the room, Mr Munch brushed Diablo's perfectly smooth fur and glared at me.

"No," I said. "I guess I haven't. Let's do this."

I gave Scout's lead to Evie, and took Mandy's. She immediately pulled in the other direction. For something so small, she was really strong.

"This way!" I said, giving her lead a tug. She skidded sideways across the wooden floor, whimpering in Evie's direction. I groaned. This was never going to work.

We finally made it to the corner of the hall with the other competitors in her heat. I was out of breath and we hadn't even started yet.

"Heel," I said and tapped her backside. She flew three feet in the air and yapped at the lady standing next to me.

"Well, I never!" the woman said, adjusting her necklace and edging away from us. I glared at Mandy.

"Sit!"

That prompt only encouraged her to scuttle away

and start sniffing at a toy poodle. I pulled her back as a man with a judge's ribbon and clipboard appeared in front of our group.

"Hello!" he said. "Our first competition today is the obedience trial. Your objective will be to summon your dog over a short distance, despite the temptation of various treats set out on either side."

Mandy's ears pricked up at the mention of the word "treat" and she began yapping excitedly and wagging her tail.

I gulped. I couldn't even get Mandy to keep still. How was I ever going to get her past a bunch of dog biscuits? This was just going from bad to worse.

And worse . . .

The judge turned a paper on his clipboard and peered over his glasses.

"First contestant," he said. "Mandy!"

CHAPTER 13

I left Mandy at the starting line, crossed my fingers she'd stay put, and took my place at the opposite end of the course. About ten metres – and half a dozen doggie treats – separated me from the bouncy Bichon Frisé. I knelt down and whistled.

"Here, Mandy!" I said.

She looked left, right, and then at me, tail wagging like mad.

"That's it!" I said. "Here girl!"

Mandy put one paw forward, but was immediately distracted by a biscuit off to the side. She sniffed the air. The judge stood over her, eyebrow raised, pen hovering above his clipboard. The lady with the fancy necklace shook her head. A couple of the other contestants sniggered. This was so not good.

"Come on, Mandy!" I said, tapping the floor.

Mandy looked back and forth again between me and the treat, and barked. I had to think of something. Mum and Dad always said I had a gift with animals. So why couldn't I get Mandy to behave? I thought about the trick I used all the time with Geronimo. It was worth a try. I had nothing else left.

I whistled a song and clicked my tongue. Mandy completely ignored me. The rest of the entrants looked at me as if I'd lost my mind. I could feel myself blushing. I tried whistling something different. One of

Freddy's nursery rhymes. Nothing. Mandy just edged closer to the biscuit. My palms began to sweat. There had to be some song that a dog would recognise!

I wiped my hands on my trousers and thought. What sort of music would Evie listen to? Something sparkly. And pink. And girly.

The Glitterati.

I could feel my face turning scarlet as I whistled their number one hit. The lyrics made my stomach turn: "Dancing in my glitter hose. Sparkly polish on my toes. You just watch me, watch me go!"

The crowd started full-on laughing at me. This was completely mortifying. But I kept at it. Mandy cocked her head to one side. I clicked my tongue and whistled louder, then tapped the floor again.

Mandy took a step forward. Then another. I continued whistling, despite the stares I could feel from the other entrants. Mandy walked faster, ignoring the treats, until she reached the last one. She slowed, head tilted to one side, and sniffed the air. Her tail wagged. I whistled louder. Mandy stuck one paw in the direction of the treat, still keeping her eyes on me.

"Oh no you don't," I said.

With a quick swipe of my arm I pulled her forward the last metre. She landed on my lap, barked, and licked my cheek.

"Good girl!" I said, rubbing her head.

The judge strode over and handed Mandy a bone-shaped biscuit. She gobbled it up eagerly and licked her paws.

"Nice work, young man," the judge said. He tapped his clipboard with the pen. "Rather a slow start there, but once you got going, it was near perfect. You've earned an eight out of ten. Congratulations!"

"Thank you," I said, breathing a sigh of relief.

The other dogs finished the round and Mandy stayed at the head of the pack. Next up were the appearance and race competitions. Mandy, being the perfectly groomed dog that she was, aced the looks round with a perfect ten score. And being such a hyper dog, she zipped through the race like she was on fire, crossing the finish line in second place.

The judge stood at the head of the group and tallied the results.

"Will the winners please join me here at the front," he said. "Third place goes to Teddy." A man with a miniature Daschund at the end of a lead walked over and stood next to the judge.

"Second place, Sydney." A boy sprang forward, grinning, a white Boxer with one blue and one brown eye lumbering behind him.

"And the winner of the heat is . . . "

I held my breath.

"Mandy!"

"Yes!" I fist-pumped the air and joined the other winners.

"Congratulations," the judge said. "You all go on to the finals! You may wait in the staging area or watch the completion of the other heats."

The group dispersed and I hurried over to see how Evie was doing with Scout.

"Hey!" I said, rushing to Evie's side. "We got first place!"

Evie and I high-fived. "How's everything going here?" I said.

"Just look." Evie smiled and pointed. The dogs were completing the last bit of the race, jumping over obstacles and charging towards the finish line. I searched for Scout, but couldn't spot him anywhere in the pack. My heart sank. Scout is super quick. He should have been right in front. I wondered what had happened to him.

"Where is he?" I said. "Did he trip up or something?" I tried to keep the disappointment out of my voice.

"No, silly," Evie said. "Look closer!" She nodded her head towards the dogs. One leapt forward ahead of the group. His fur was all smooth and shiny. A sleek collar was fastened around his neck and a pair of blue and green ribbons hung from behind his ears, trailing in the air as he jumped. A far cry from the mangy, dirt-covered scruffball I'd shown up with. I barely recognised him.

"Scout?" I said.

Evie grinned. "I gave him a little makeover."

"Wow," was all I could manage to say. Poor Scout

looked kind of ridiculous. At least the ribbons weren't pink.

Scout crossed the finish line in first place and bounded over to me, tail wagging.

"Well done, boy!" I said, rubbing behind his ears. Was that perfume I could smell? I was about to ask Evie when the loudspeaker crackled and the judge began announcing the winners of Scout's heat. My stomach did little flips as Scout's name was read – just barely coming in at third place.

"That's great," Evie said, tapping my arm.

"Yeah, I s'pose," I said. I swallowed hard and looked at all the dogs left in the competition. Pure bred Dobermans and Great Danes and Fox Terriers, each properly groomed and pedigreed. Then, there was Diablo. Virtually invincible. It was going to take everything we had to beat him.

148

And as much as I hated to admit it, our best shot wasn't Scout.

"Look," I said to Evie. "If either of our dogs is going to win this thing, it's going to be Mandy."

Evie's eyebrows shot up. "Oh, I wouldn't say that," she said, uncharacteristically modest. "Scout's awesome! He actually sat still while I combed his hair. Mandy never does that."

"Yeah," I said. "But no matter how many ribbons and bows you put on him, he's still a mongrel." Scout whined, almost as if he knew what I was saying. I rubbed his head. "It's OK, boy. I love you. You're still the best dog in my book. But Mandy's got all the right papers and breeding. And if we're going to win this, we need to work together. Focus all our efforts on getting her in first place."

Evie scooped up Mandy and adjusted her hair ribbons. "Are you sure, Leo?" she said.

149

"Yeah, I'm positive."

Evie straightened the bows in her own hair. "Thanks," she said. "But listen, if we win, this was a team effort. We split the prize, OK? And all bets are off."

I grinned. "Looks like Scout's already had that makeover anyway."

The loudspeaker crackled on.

"Contestants!" a voice said. "Please make your way to the centre of the hall. The finals will begin in five minutes!"

Evie put Mandy back on the ground.

"It's show time, girl!" she said.

But just then, Mandy began to twitch. Her tongue lolled from her mouth and she panted loudly. She clawed the floor and walked in circles, hyper-ventilating.

"Mandy?" Evie said. "What's the matter?" She leaned down.

"Maybe she's just nervous?" I said hopefully. But I wasn't too sure. The only time I'd ever seen Scout act like this was when he ate the squeaker out of a chewy toy. He paced up and down all day until he finally puked it up.

Evie reached out to touch Mandy, but before she could, the little dog collapsed on her side, unmoving. Evie shrieked and scooped her up.

"Mandy, Mandy." She frantically rubbed her fur. The dog's stomach rose and fell in short bursts. Her eyes stayed closed and her mouth hung open, tongue flopping out sideways. She was really ill. I searched the room for help. My eyes landed on Mr Munch, who stood in the corner watching us, a blood-red smirk on his gaunt face. He held a box of dog biscuits in the air.

I shivered as I realised it was the same kind Mandy had eaten at the end of the obedience course. Mr Munch gave the box a little shake, then ran his hand across his neck in a slicing motion.

"The biscuit!" I said.

"What biscuit?" Evie said, tears squeezing from the corners of her eyes.

"She ate one of Mr Munch's biscuits," I said. "It must have been poisoned. You've got to get her to a vet—"

But at the word "poisoned", Evie was already gone, running towards the door with Mandy flopped sideways in her arms. Across the room, Mr Munch watched with a thin-lipped smile. He adjusted his top hat and winked at me. A chill ran the full length of my spine. The man was evil. Pure evil.

And I was going to stop him.

CHAPTER 14

I took my place in the line-up for the finals. There were nine dogs competing, including Diablo. The other animals all gave Mr Munch's dog a wide berth, except for one – a fierce-looking Doberman Pinscher. Diablo turned and growled at it, eyes blazing. The dog whimpered, tucked its tail in, and slinked away.

This was going to be impossible.

Mayor Feversham stepped onto a small podium in

front of an obstacle course and tapped the microphone. The crowd fell silent, except for the odd bark.

"Greetings, ladies and gentlemen!" the mayor said. "We have reached the exciting conclusion of our competition here today! Our last challenge will be a race to the finish – winner takes all." He swept his hand over the track before him. It had been laid out with hurdles to jump, tunnels to go through, and platforms to traverse. A ripple of applause went through the spectators.

"Competitors, to your places!" he said.

I led Scout to the starting line. Diablo and Mr Munch stood directly to my right.

"Prepared to lose?" Mr Munch leaned over and sneered in my ear.

"Are you?" I shot back. "Scout could run circles around your dog."

"I didn't mean the race," Mr Munch said. "I meant, your *life.*"

My mouth went dry. "You're going to pay for what you did to Mandy and those other animals," I said with a gulp.

Mr Munch cackled. "I think you mean, I'll *get* paid . . . " he said. "Sales of PetMunch will go through the roof after today."

I remembered how he'd kicked Scout in the factory. It took everything I had not to punch him in the nose right then and there.

The mayor stood at the front of the line and held a starting pistol above his head. "On your marks, get set, go!" He pulled the trigger. The gun popped and the dogs took off. The crowd cheered.

"Go, Scout, go!" I yelled.

Scout raced off as quickly as his legs would take

him, leaping over a hurdle and dodging an obstacle. He was making great time.

But Diablo was too fast. He already had a metre's lead, just seconds into the race.

"On second thoughts, I'm glad I didn't put your mongrel into my latest batch," Mr Munch said. "His inferior skills would only have slowed Diablo down."

I could feel my temper boil. I had to stay focused on what mattered right now – winning the race. I walked to the side of the course, where the dogs were charging around the corner. Diablo was still in front, mouth hanging open. I could've sworn he actually smirked at me as he passed. As he did, I noticed that chipped tooth, the one that looked just like Geronimo's.

Suddenly it hit me. Maybe that wasn't the only thing he had in common with my hamster ...

I clicked my tongue and whistled. But none of that

ridiculous Glitterati stuff. This time I used my favourite song, "Dog Eat Dog" by The Mongrels.

The song I trained Geronimo to.

Diablo slowed and his ears pricked up.

"Roll over!" I yelled.

The dog dropped to the ground and flipped upside down.

"What are you doing, Diablo?" Mr Munch yelled. "Go!"

Diablo popped back up and raced off again. He was still in front, but Scout was getting closer. I whistled and clicked again.

"Beg!" I said.

Diablo sat and put his paws in the air.

"Diablo!" Mr Munch yelled.

The dog scrambled to his feet and charged forward. My plan was working, but not well enough. I needed something that would slow Diablo down enough to let Scout win the race. I pictured Geronimo – rolling over, begging . . .

Hang on! That was it!

I grinned, pursed my lips and whistled loudly.

"Chase your tail!" It was Geronimo's best trick. He could do it for hours.

Diablo screeched to a stop, spotted his own wagging tail and ran in circles after it. Mr Munch hovered at the side of the course. "The finish line!" he yelled, his face nearly purple. "Get over the finish line! What are you *doing*?"

But it was no use. Diablo just kept barking and chasing after himself, without another care in the world. Some of the spectators began to point and laugh. Scout charged up from behind, jumped over a hurdle and sailed past him.

"Go, Scout!" I jumped up and down, cheering. "Go! Go! Go!"

I was nearly out of breath with excitement as my dog ran through a tunnel and across the finish line in first place. I ran, knelt down, and wrapped my arms around his neck. He licked me happily. The spectators broke out in applause.

"You did it, boy! You did it!" I said. I couldn't imagine a better moment in my life.

But then, the hall went eerily silent, except for a random whimper.

I looked up from Scout's muzzle. Mr Munch was standing over me, that antique pistol aimed right at my head.

"You cheated!" he spat, face red with rage. His narrow tie was twisted sideways and the veins in his neck bulged. He turned, gun swinging to the side. The

159

crowd ducked. "He cheated!" Mr Munch yelled again.

I stood slowly, hands over my head. "Hey, look," I said. "Let's be reasonable."

"Reasonable?" Mr Munch said. "The only reasonable solution is to declare Diablo the winner." He looked back at his dog, still running in circles. "Make! Him! Stop!" he said.

"Yes, sir," I said. I let out one long, low whistle. Diablo came to an immediate halt and sat.

"You," Mr Munch said, pointing the gun at me again, "are going to pay for everything you've done!"

I swallowed hard.

"But first," he said. "I'm going to take care of that mangy dog of yours!" He turned the pistol on Scout.

"No!" I wrapped my arms around Scout and pinched my eyes shut.

There was a loud bang. But it wasn't the gun. It was

the hall doors opening. I looked up to see the police bursting in, Evie right behind them, with Mandy in her arms.

Mr Munch turned towards the commotion. I seized the opportunity to kick the gun from his hands. It skidded across the floor. Two officers ran to Mr Munch, twisted his arms behind his back, and, before he could react, slapped on a pair of handcuffs. Another retrieved the weapon and stood before Mr Munch.

"You are under arrest," he said, "for the poisoning of this dog in an attempt to fraudulently win the dog show." He pointed at Mandy.

"Wait! I'm not the cheat!" Mr Munch wailed. "He is!" He tried to motion in my direction, but the cuffs around his wrists made it impossible to move. He squirmed as the police led him out of the hall.

Evie sidled up next to me. Scout rubbed his muzzle against my leg. I patted Mandy's head.

"I'm so glad she's OK," I said.

"Yeah, there was a vet on site and he got her to, you know, work that poisoned biscuit back out," she said with a shudder. "I definitely don't need to see that again. Ever. Ewwww!"

"Glad you're both back to normal," I said with a smile. "That's all that matters."

Sirens wailed outside. I listened as they faded away.

"How long do you think they can hold him for poisoning Mandy?" I said. "What do we do if he's back out in a week?"

"Well," Evie said. "I wouldn't be too worried about that."

"No?"

"No," she said. "I also told the police that *poison*

wasn't all he was putting in his dog food. That they might want to check his factory. Word is that brotherly envy might have got the better of him, if you know what I mean . . . "

"That's brilliant," I said. "He'll never be able to explain how Mr Fortescue ended up in the PetMunch!"

"Exactly," Evie grinned. "I think it's safe to say we've seen the last of Mr Munch!"

CHAPTER 15

I grabbed a bag of crisps and plopped down next to Evie on the sofa. Mandy was curled on her lap, Scout sat at my feet and Freddy was over in the corner, gnawing on a cardboard box.

"D'you think he's gonna be OK?" Evie said, nodding towards my brother, who was now snarling at his own backside.

"Don't know," I said. "The doctor couldn't work out

what was wrong with him. Just gave Mum some cream to get rid of the hair."

"I don't think it's working," Evie said as Freddy scratched a tuft of fur on his cheek.

I began to wonder if my brother was going to turn into an actual dog. After all, the little furbrain was halfway there even *before* he ate the dog food.

Evie pulled a black envelope from her pocket and began counting the money inside. "That's fifty pounds for you," she said. "And fifty for me." I shoved the cash in my pocket. Evie turned the envelope over and over, inspecting it.

"What is it?" I said.

"Just wondered, why black?" she said. "Sort of an odd colour choice, don't you think?"

I shrugged. "Yeah, well, welcome to Weirdsville," I said. Evie laughed.

I switched on the TV and held out the crisps to Evie. Mandy immediately jumped up and stuck her nose in the bag.

"Down, girl!" Evie said. Mandy ignored her.

I whistled The Glitterati, clicked my tongue, and said, "Sit!" Mandy settled down on Evie's lap.

"You know, Leo, that was actually pretty cool," Evie said. "Maybe you could teach me how to do that."

"Um, sure," I nodded. I could feel the tips of my ears going red. The TV screen flickered. I cleared my throat and pointed. "Look, the news is about to come on."

Evie turned quickly to the TV. The newsreader appeared on the screen, an image of Weirville town hall to the right of his head.

"It was more than just the usual tricks, treats, and races yesterday at the Annual Weirville Dog Show," he

166

said. "Reclusive pet food magnate Herman Munch –
AKA Herman Fortescue – threatened a young entrant
with a gun after Munch's dog, Diablo, lost in the final
competition." A camera-phone video of Mr Munch,
waving his pistol in the air, flashed on the screen.
"Munch is also suspected of poisoning another
entrant who ... "

The newsreader stopped and adjusted his earpiece.

"One minute, please," he said. "We have some
breaking news." He nodded and scribbled something
on the paper in front of him. A red "News Flash"
graphic replaced the video. "I am getting reports that
human remains – I repeat, human remains – have
been found in the dog food at PetMunch's Weirville
factory." The blood had drained from the newsreader's
face.

Evie turned to me, and we high-fived.

"And there's more," the newsreader continued.

"More?" Evie said. We both looked back at the TV.

"We are also receiving reports that Mr Munch has escaped custody," the newsreader said, eyebrows furrowed.

Escaped?

My heartbeat began to drum loudly in my ears. I turned up the volume so I could hear over the sound.

"The police say that Munch is armed and dangerous." The newsreader glanced off-camera to his right. "Can I have that footage again?" he said. The video of Mr Munch waving his gun popped back on the screen. Scout growled at the TV. Mandy tucked her head on Evie's chest and whimpered.

"This is the suspect," the newsreader continued. "If you see him, call the police immediately. Do not approach him. I repeat, he is considered armed and dangerous. Do not attempt to apprehend him yourself. And whatever you do, do not feed your dog PetMunch!"

I clicked off the TV and jumped from the sofa. The house was eerily quiet. Dad was still at work and Mum had gone to the supermarket.

We were alone.

"I'm sure it's OK," Evie said with a shaking voice. "I mean, he wouldn't come here, would he? He's got to be halfway to Brazil by now."

"Yeah," I gulped. "Brazil ... "

Outside, tyres crunched across the gravel driveway. Evie raced to the window and peered through the curtains. She let out a small squeak and slapped her hand over her mouth. I rushed to her side and looked out.

Sitting in the driveway was a beaten-up old black

van. The one from the cemetery. The driver's door flew open.

"We've got to get out of here!" I said.

We raced down the hall, Scout and Mandy at our heels, just as the chime of the doorbell echoed through the house. I scanned my options. Upstairs was no good. We'd be trapped. And the police would never get here in time.

A wild banging began on the front door.

"Open up!" Mr Munch yelled. "It's time to pay the piper." I could hear the knob rattling. Evie screamed.

Dread and panic washed over me. My legs froze. For a moment, I felt like I was stuck in one of those dreams where you can't move. Or speak. My breath came out in short bursts. Scout barked and nudged the back of my knees with his muzzle. I snapped out of it and rubbed his head. "Thanks, boy."

"This way," I said, leading Evie and the dogs through the kitchen and out of the back door. "We can go through the garden to the neighbour's."

We hurried down the back steps and into the garden. We were halfway across the lawn when Evie's foot got caught in a hole. She tumbled to the ground.

"Ow!" she moaned, grabbing her ankle. I reached down and helped her up. She hopped on one foot, gripping my hand.

"I think I sprained it," she said with a grimace.

I wrapped my arm around her waist. She leaned on me and lurched forward, wincing with every step. We hobbled to the edge of my garden. But now we had another problem.

The fence!

We came to a dead stop in front of the two-metre

tall wooden structure. Evie glanced up. "There's no way I can get over that thing with my foot."

"The dogs would never make it, either," I said.

Evie gulped. "Maybe you should go. Get help."

"No way," I said. "I'm not leaving you guys here. We'll think of something else."

I turned back around in time to see Mr Munch striding up the side path. His red overcoat and top hat were gone, replaced by a simple blue prison uniform. His slick black hair was dishevelled and he carried a horrible metal contraption that looked like a giant corkscrew. He stopped at the back door, holding the thing above his head, and gave it a crank. He hadn't seen us in the garden.

"Oh, bad little children!" he said, face close to the door. "Time to come out and meet this wonderful device my brother invented. Works perfectly for getting the meat out of an animal before stuffing it!"

Evie trembled beneath my arm. We held our breath for a long moment.

"What?" he bellowed. "The three of you don't want to come out and play? Why not? I think you'd all look wonderful, stuffed and mounted in Fortescue's Curiosities, next to your little mongrels!" He laughed madly.

The three of us? What did that mean?

"Oh, no!" I suddenly realised. "Freddy!" He was still in the house. How could I have left him there?

Evie's face turned pale. I slipped my hand from her waist and ran forward. "Get away from my house, you madman!" I yelled.

Mr Munch spun around, eyes wild. "Why, there you are!" His thin lips curled upward. He strode towards me, grinding the corkscrew. "Don't worry, this will only hurt for a minute . . . or ten! Depends whether we go in through the ear or the nose. Really, any soft spot will do . . . "

My stomach lurched. I looked around for something to overpower him with. All I saw was a stupid plastic garden gnome. Where was a rock when I needed one? Then I spotted a furry shape coming out of the back door on all fours, head down, snarling. Scout?

No.

Freddy!

I whistled and my brother's head cocked to one side. "Attack!" I yelled.

With a loud woof, Freddy cannonballed down the back steps and landed on Mr Munch's back, knocking him flat on the ground and sending the corkscrew flying. Scout and Mandy charged over, growling, and hopped on top of him. I grabbed the corkscrew and held it over his head.

"So how did you say this thing works?" I said, giving it a twist. "Any old soft spot will do?"

Mr Munch tried to lift his shoulder. "Let me go, you infernal brats!" he said.

"Sure, we'll let you go." Evie hobbled over and forced him back down, pressing her good foot onto his chest.

"Straight to prison," I said.

Mr Munch groaned. "Don't think I can't get out a second time," he said.

"Not likely," I said. "They'll have you in a straitjacket this time. But don't worry. I'm sure you'll love jail. At least the food will be better than PetMunch!"

CHAPTER 16

Darkness had fallen by the time the police had taken our statements. Mum, Evie, Freddy and I were in the living room having tea. The blue lights of the police car flashed across the wall as it pulled away, Mr Munch handcuffed in the back.

"I'm still in shock, Leo," Mum said. "What did that man want with you, anyway?"

"Long story," I said. "Let's just say he wasn't happy Scout won the show yesterday."

"Quite the sore loser," Mum said. She reached over and patted Freddy's head. He wagged it back and forth in appreciation. "And what a brave little boy you are. Attacking that bad man like a ferocious guard dog!"

Freddy woofed. Mum laughed. My brother sank back on his haunches, curled his lips and snarled.

I shook my head. If only Mum knew how right she was . . .

Mum picked up a plate from the table. "Oh, looks like we're almost out of biscuits!" she said. Mandy's ears pricked up at the sound of her favourite word. "Let me get some more," Mum said.

She headed into the kitchen. I leaned back and sipped my tea. I was so glad this mess was finally over. I was quite sure the police weren't going to let Mr Munch slip out of their clutches this time. I smiled at Evie. She half-smiled back. But her face was still pale.

"Are you OK?" I said. "Ankle sore?"

She adjusted the ice pack Mum had given her and shifted around in her seat. "No," she said. "It's not that."

"Then what's the matter? We got the Munch twins. We even got the prize."

"I know," she said. "It's just there's something missing ..." She bit her lip. Her voice dropped to a whisper, as if she barely dared to say the word out loud. "... Diablo."

"Oh." My chest tightened. "Right. *Diablo.*"

He's still out there. Somewhere.

One by one, the hairs on the back of my neck stood on end. I was struck by the weird feeling that someone – or something – was watching me. I got up and walked to the window.

The garden was cast in darkness, so it was hard to see anything.

I reached for the edges of the curtains. As I drew them slowly closed, I saw two points of red, peering from the bushes near the back fence.

"Evie," I called, my breath catching in my throat.

"What is it, Leo?" she said, coming over.

I lifted my hand to point, but the red eyes had vanished. Maybe they'd never been there at all. The bush *was* rustling a bit, but it was probably just the wind.

"Oh, nothing," I said. "I'm just seeing things."

I hope.

WELCOME TO
WEIRDSVILLE

Happyland

Don't miss the first
Welcome to Weirdsville book
Happyland!

Read on for an extract ...

Tickets. Jet black like the envelope, the words the same sticky blood red as the handwriting on the front.

"This must be a joke," I muttered. I looked over my shoulder and around the pier. But there was no one else in sight. Not a single friend, or enemy.

The place was dead.

"Maybe," Emma said. "But it's sooooo cool!" She snatched a ticket and stretched it out in front of her face. "A midnight visit to Happyland? That's a seriously awesome birthday present. And who was that clown? He was pretty freaky, right?"

"Hmmmm," Lucas said. "I don't think I want to know. Maybe those tickets are actually meant for someone else."

"Someone called Toby?" Emma said, eyebrow raised.

"There's got to be more than one Toby in Weirville . . . " Lucas countered.

"With a birthday today?" Emma said.

"Could be," Lucas said.

"An *eleventh* birthday?" Emma pointed at the card with the big 11 on it, then crossed her arms and tapped her foot.

"Well, uh . . . " Lucas tailed off.

Emma was right. If it was a coincidence, it was a pretty huge one.

I glanced at my watch just as the minute hand twitched to twelve. Suddenly I remembered – we were going to be late.

"Come on," I said. "Mum wanted us home at four."

"Where do you losers think you're going?" Keira yelled as we started to walk back. She blocked our way, planting her hands on her hips.

"Home," I told her.

"Not yet you're not." She thrust out her hand. "First I want my ticket."

"*Your* ticket?" I said.

"Yeah, *genius*, my ticket. There are four tickets and four of us. One each." She scowled at me.

I scowled back. "Are you going to leave us alone if I give you one?"

"Like I want to hang around with you."

I peeled a ticket from my hand and shoved it into hers. "Fine," I said. "Bye, Keira."

"Yeah, see you at midnight. Unless you're too scared." She raised her arms and staggered around like a zombie, tongue lolling, then stuffed the ticket in her pocket and ran away cackling.

"What a cow," Lucas muttered, once she was well out of earshot.

I nodded. "Come on," I said. "Mum's made cake."

As we walked down the pier, I took one look back at the deserted Happyland. It hung over us like a dark cloud in an otherwise sunny sky. Nothing moved except a torn candyfloss banner that flapped helplessly against an empty snack stand. Of all the places for my ball to land. The fiery pits of hell would've been more welcoming.